T5-BAO-261

"Accept my apology for stepping on a sore nerve?" Nick asked, offering her his hand.

In a weak moment, Carla took it. Nick pulled her to him, curling his other hand around the back of her neck, and covered her mouth with a kiss.

She could no more have stopped herself from melting against him than she could levitate. Needs she'd tried to bury flashed to life with a ferocity that frightened her.

"Nick, stop," she said. "I don't want this . . ." Her voice trailed off as every fiber of her body begged her to say yes to all he was asking.

"Yes, you do, sweetheart. I can feel the very beat of your heart crying out for me. It's thrumming in the air around us. Feel it? You can tell I'm starving for you, can't you?"

Yes, and she was starving too. "Nick—"

"Give up the battle, love, because sooner or later you're going to surrender and have me. It's fated. . . ."

WHAT ARE *LOVESWEPT* ROMANCES?

They are stories of true romance and touching emotion. We believe those two very important ingredients are constants in our highly sensual and very believable stories in the *LOVESWEPT* line. Our goal is to give you, the reader, stories of consistently high quality that may sometimes make you laugh, sometimes make you cry, but are always fresh and creative and contain many delightful surprises within their pages.

Most romance fans read an enormous number of books. Those they truly love, they keep. Others may be traded with friends and soon forgotten. We hope that each *LOVESWEPT* romance will be a treasure—a "keeper." We will always try to publish

LOVE STORIES YOU'LL NEVER FORGET
BY AUTHORS YOU'LL ALWAYS REMEMBER

The Editors

Loveswept®598

Joan J. Domning
The Forever Man

BANTAM BOOKS
NEW YORK · TORONTO · LONDON · SYDNEY · AUCKLAND

THE FOREVER MAN
A Bantam Book / February 1993

LOVESWEPT® *and the wave design are registered*
trademarks of Bantam Books, a division of
Bantam Doubleday Dell Publishing Group, Inc.
Registered in U.S. Patent
and Trademark Office and elsewhere.

All rights reserved.
Copyright © 1993 by Joan J. Domning.
Cover art copyright © 1993 by Hal Frenck.
No part of this book may be reproduced or transmitted
in any form or by any means, electronic or mechanical,
including photocopying, recording, or by any
information storage and retrieval system, without
permission in writing from the publisher.
For information address: Bantam Books.

If you purchased this book without a cover you should be
aware that this book is stolen property. It was reported as
"unsold and destroyed" to the publisher and neither the
author nor the publisher has received any payment for this
"stripped book."

If you would be interested in receiving protective vinyl
covers for your Loveswept books, please write to this address
for information:

Loveswept
Bantam Books
P.O. Box 985
Hicksville, NY 11802

ISBN 0-553-44365-8

Published simultaneously in the United States and Canada

Bantam Books are published by Bantam Books, a division of
Bantam Doubleday Dell Publishing Group, Inc. Its trademark,
consisting of the words "Bantam Books" and the portrayal of
a rooster, is Registered in U.S. Patent and Trademark Office
and in other countries. Marca Registrada. Bantam Books, 666
Fifth Avenue, New York, New York 10103.

PRINTED IN THE UNITED STATES OF AMERICA

OPM   0 9 8 7 6 5 4 3 2 1

For my daughter with the lovely smile, Stephanie, and her Steve, the wilderness trekkers.

One

It was almost six P.M. before Carla Hudson waved the other stylists off and closed Hudson's Hair. Her feet ached and she longed to go home too. Instead, she grimly tucked her western blouse into her jeans and sat down at the desk to tackle the June bills.

Balancing the salon budget was a snap compared to unraveling her great-aunt's ranch books. The old woman had waltzed into an unclarified lease as worrisome as her debts, pooh-poohing Carla's warnings. Granted, the lump sum of six months' rent from Wilderness Enterprises, Inc. had covered the more urgent bills, but she mistrusted what the out-of-state company meant to do with the ranch. "I do love you, Grace, but really!" she muttered with an exasperated laugh.

Completely engrossed, she hadn't heard the door open, and nearly jumped out of her skin when a large, tanned fist rapped on the desk for attention. "Talking to yourself is bad enough, but laughing . . . ?"

A shiver shot down Carla's spine. Jerking up her head, she gaped at the tall man. He looked like a desperado.

The lower half of his face was hidden by a bushy black beard, the upper by a limp hat with two feathers sprouting up in front. A stained, fringed buckskin shirt hung over his hips, belted by a red sash. She guessed he might be one of the prospectors who still poked around the Montana mountains. But what did he want in her beauty salon?

Coming to her senses, Carla snapped her mouth shut and glanced out the window. The stores along Main Street were still open and folks were passing on the sidewalk. "What can I do for you?" she asked, knowing rescue was only a scream away if necessary.

Tossing the hat on a chair, he undid his ponytail and released a mop of wild black hair. "How about a haircut?"

Without the hat, his midnight-dark eyes looked sane enough, but the built-in sexy sparkle was unsettling. A woman alone couldn't be too careful. "Sorry, I'm closed."

"Are you Carla Hudson?"

"I . . . well . . . yes, I guess," she said cautiously.

"Then I'm no stranger to you. I'm Nicholas Leclerc."

His name had a familiar ring; she repeated it as she'd heard it, hoping to jog her memory. "Nicholas Leclare . . . ?"

"Just Nick would be fine." A flirty white grin flashed through his beard. "Or Nicky, if you happen to be feeling cozy, warm, and pliable."

Carla stiffened: The man was coming on to her! "I don't feel pliable, and you don't look a bit familiar, Mr. Leclerc, so . . ." She glanced pointedly toward the door.

"Oh, please—just a haircut. I'm flying home in the morning, and they may let me on the plane up in Missoula looking like this, but I doubt they'll let me off at LAX."

Her brows shot up under tousled chestnut bangs. "If you're from Los Angeles, what are you doing in that getup?"

The teasing sparkle of his eyes wrapped itself

around her. "I won't tell you unless you cut my hair."

Curiosity toppled her better senses. "I don't suppose any homicidal maniac would run around looking as weird as you do," she said, walking across the squeaky floor to her station. Lush vines hung around the mirror, and the styling chair she swung around was almost antique. "Have a seat; let's find out if you're salvageable."

He walked toward her, a man in prime, muscular shape under his appalling outfit, so tall and broad-shouldered, he had trouble fitting himself into the chair. "Thank you, ma'am," he said, grinning. "Your heart is pure gold."

"Don't count on that." She matched his cocky grin with one of her own. "It's after hours, so this haircut is going to cost you plenty. I hope you can afford it . . . what did you say you name is?"

"Nicky." Giving a chuckling, infectious laugh, he hooked the heels of his boots on the footrest and let his knees drop apart. "And all yours, so be gentle, okay?"

His flip plea and blatant display sent a tingle of response through her body. She'd thought she was immune; hadn't she laid hands on some of the sexiest men in Hollywood in her time, and never blinked an eye? She whipped a pink cape over his body, but that didn't protect her from the seductive feral aroma of his buckskin shirt, or the freshly bathed and shampooed scent of the man himself.

She began to realize it wasn't this wildman she should mistrust, but herself. Taking a deep breath for control, she ran professional fingers into his long hair, testing for cowlicks and texture. "How do you want it cut?"

"Just take a bunch off."

"Shorter or longer than mine?" She touched her boyishly cut chestnut hair and glanced at him in the mirror.

Nick was gazing back as if smitten. She'd never

cared for the pixieish look of her high cheekbones, widely spaced violet eyes, and pointed chin, but it wasn't slowing him down. "What style do *you* like on your men?" he asked, his voice deepening.

"What possible difference could my opinion make?"

"I thought maybe if you do me up into something you like, I can talk you into . . . uh . . . whooping it up after we're finished here." His grin was a challenge.

The responses in her body were ridiculous; the man was a stranger! Carla backed away from the chair. "If you've got what I think you've got on your mind, buddy, then you're talking to the *wrong* hair-stylist. You better leave."

His expression turned apologetic. "Sorry, that was out of line. Let me explain that I've been running around in the wilderness and haven't seen a woman for two months. When you turned out to be such a pretty lady, I began wallowing in fantasies, I guess. But I swear I'm not so desperate I'd jump you. Please, let me stay. I need that haircut."

His gaze was so sincere, she conceded. "Well . . . okay. But keep those fantasies buried in your head, because if they branch out to your fingertips, you're out of here." She eyed him for a second, then walked back to the chair. "All right, how do you want your hair cut?"

That sparkle fired his eyes again. "Tenderly."

His cheekiness surprised a laugh out of her. "Okay, that's it—you get generic."

Flipping up the counter that covered the sink, she wet him down, toweled him, fought the tangles into submission, and combed his long hair over his face. "Which wilderness have you been running around in?" she asked, tilting his head to expose one ear with a few scissor snips.

"The Selway-Bitterroot, west of here. I followed the Salmon River from just south of Oregon to Idaho, where I left it to come north into the Bitterroot Valley."

She began layering the back of his head, showering heavy hair to the floor. "If I recall my map, that area is a couple hundred miles of the worst kind of mountains, and no roads. Not to be a skeptic, but you can't really expect me to believe you crossed that alone."

"I never suggested I did it alone. I had a crew, radio contact with the outside, and supplies helicoptered in. I'm a photographer, under contract to a nature magazine for an article with stills and a film for television about a trail the beaver trappers used in the eighteen hundreds. My business is nature films. I really wanted to shoot a primitive tribe of Amazon rain forest Indians—but they had other ideas, so I did this one instead, on horseback with pack mules. It was a bitch, but it made for damn good footage."

She glanced at his reflection. "Good Lord, when you first came in I thought you were a vagrant prospector."

A grin burst through his beard. "You were close to right. I'm a vagrant camera bum with nothing but my base of operations in Los Angeles to call my own."

Frowning, Carla tilted his head to snip the other ear into view. He seemed intelligent and aggressive enough to choose that kind of lifestyle, or any other he wanted; so why did she sense a loneliness under his surface? She'd felt that way often enough herself to recognize it in others. It drew her to him.

Facing Nick with a hip braced on the arm of the chair, she began shaping the top of his hair. Her position put her disturbingly within his personal space. His eyes were closed against the fall of snippets, but she could feel awareness crackling in the air between them. His breathing sounded ragged in the silence, and hers quickened in response.

"Your ratty old hat and buckskin shirt don't seem to jibe with helicopters and Los Angeles," she blurted out, breaking the spell with the first thought that came to mind.

Nick shifted restlessly and propped one ankle over the other leg, knee jutting through a thready hole in his jeans. "Oh, that. I'm a stickler for authenticity, and I'm French, so I dressed up as a voyageur—the French peons who did grunt labor for the trappers—buckskins, red sash, and a blue frock coat. My coat, unhappily, got washed down the river."

"Fascinating," Carla murmured, more interested in the features she'd snipped into view: high cheekbones, an eagle's beak of a nose, two black slashes for brows, the left one scarred. His beard gave his face such an outrageously virile look, she couldn't resist asking about his personal life. "If you've been on the trail since April, I can believe you're eager to fly back to your family and . . . wife?"

Nick squinted devilish eyes against the snippets caught in his long lashes. "No wife, no kids, no ties. Do you have a husband, fiancé, boyfriend?"

She gave an embarrassed laugh over being caught. "No, and I only asked because I'm nosy, so don't get any ideas."

"I already have a ton of 'em," he said, his mellow voice curling around her. "And I'm not anxious to go home. I told you, I'm a camera bum, addicted to roving."

Since he'd felt the need to repeat it, she suspected his declaration was an attempt to convince himself. "Hold still, I want to check the lay of the land," she said, angling herself awkwardly between his jutting knee and torso to look at his face head-on. Scowling intently, she ran fingers through his hair, checking for tag ends.

"From where I sit," Nick said in a velvety voice, "the lay of the land looks very, very nice."

Glancing at him, Carla found his heated, dark gaze aimed down the deep V neck of her plaid blouse, probing the valley between her breasts. Jerking back, she clapped her hand over the scorched area, giving him an exasperated look. "It takes either a very brave or a very stupid man to provoke a woman with a pair of scissors in her hand. Which are you?"

"I thought we agreed fantasies were acceptable," he said with a sassy grin.

"I didn't agree to anything but a haircut," she said, brushing off his face and neck with a whisk broom. "And you're sheared now."

Nick turned his head this way and that, peering in the mirror at his hair; it was wavy and disciplined on the sides and top, longer and curling at the nape of the neck. "Didn't I hear you threaten me with generic? This is better than any cut I've gotten in Southern California."

"That's because I'm not there any longer," Carla murmured modestly, flushing with pleasure over his praise. "I used to do hair in a Hollywood makeup crew for various film companies."

His brows shot up. "I'll be damned! I've done camera work for the big screen off and on over the years."

Carla leaned her hips against the counter. "It seems an odd coincidence, you turning up here."

His lips twitched in a secretive smile. "Not really."

"Why? Have we worked on a shoot together? Is that why you thought I should know you when you first came in?"

"I don't remember that we have, to my loss." Nick removed his ankle from his knee and shifted upright in the chair. "Have you ever met Bunny Fletcher or Preston Mann?"

Film crews lived a nomadic life, moving here and there, wherever work could be found; everyone either knew, or had heard of, each other. "I don't recall Bunny, but I knew Preston well. He was the assistant director on a couple of films I did hair for, and he also dated my sister for a while, before . . ." She shook the sad memory off. "Why?"

"Pres is producing his own films now, environmental stuff. Bunny works for me—or runs me—and we collaborate with him sometimes. I've written a screenplay, and if all goes as I hope, he'll film it for me."

"That's nice," she said, painfully aware that half of the people in Hollywood talked about having a script filmed or becoming a star, a director, whatever. So few ever caught the lucky brass ring. Skirting the subject, she asked, "Did you ever meet . . ."

After an orgy of "do you knows" and "do you remembers," Nick asked, "How long since you switched to civilian life?"

"I came back and started my business about three years ago." Carla glanced proudly around the somewhat shabby but sparkling-clean salon, a veritable greenhouse with all the plants hanging from the ceiling. "It's been a modest success, if I do say so myself."

He studied her curiously. "I find it hard to believe you earn even a fraction as much as you did in the industry. Why'd you leave a successful career for this?"

"Lots of reasons—to get away from the smog, the traffic, the seething mass of humanity." Picking up a brush, she thumbed the bristles and grazed against the real reason: "Not to mention the sex and drug culture."

Afraid he'd probe, she said quickly, "I guess I really came back because the Bitterroot Valley is the only place I've ever thought of as home. My sister and I lived with my great-aunt on the family ranch for a few years when we were kids. It hasn't changed since then. I like things stable."

"It's stable, all right." He glanced out the window. The sun was going down in flames behind rugged mountains, bathing the genuine, old west buildings in a ruddy glow. Everything was closed up tight at seven; not a soul was in sight. "I've heard of picking up the sidewalks for the night, but this place has rolled over and played dead. It reminds me of something out of *Twilight Zone*."

"Then it's a good thing no one's forcing you to stay, camera bum." Carla circled the chair, reaching out for the pink cape. "You're all finished, so-o-o . . ."

"Wait, I've still got a problem." Nick unearthed a hand to tug at his beard. "Now that you've tamed my hair this thing looks like a rabid steel wool pad."

She lifted her brows. "What do you intend to do about it?"

"I'll have to trim it, or shave it." He glanced at her full lips, his eyes sparkling a challenge. "In your opinion, is a man more kissable with or without?"

She went hot, because the question had been ripe in her mind. "I wouldn't know, I've never kissed a man with a beard." Which was a perfect cue for him to purse his lips invitingly. "And I have absolutely no intention of kissing you to find out," she added hastily.

He laughed, snapping his fingers. "Nuts! Oh, well, I think I'll opt for clean-shaven, but I'm not sure how to get this thing off. Are you?"

"I've shaved my share of beards over the years." With an eye to fighting banter with banter, Carla rummaged in a drawer for a straight razor she hadn't used for ages, and began honing it on a leather strop. "Are you game?"

Nick looked at her impish face and lifted a brow. "I doubt a serial killer would go around looking as diabolical as you do with that thing, so have at me."

She laughed and shot back, "Before we get started, let me clarify that a haircut is one thing, but a shave is going to cost you another arm and leg."

"Agreed—I haven't seen my face for two months, and I'm dying to find out what's under the foliage."

Carla was too; she trimmed his beard down to the skin with the scissors, spread lather, and began wielding the razor with adept enthusiasm, exposing lean cheeks and an angular jaw. After reaming out a rather cunning dimple in his square chin, she stood back, shaken breathless by the dynamic energy in the face she'd bared.

"So . . . ?" he murmured, reading her reaction. "What's the verdict? Am I more kissable without the beard?"

"The verdict is—your face looks very tan on top and pretty anemic on the bottom," she said lightly; it'd be lethal to admit how attractive she found him. "But you do clean up real nice."

His cocky grin was far more seductive without the beard. "Does that mean you feel warm, pliable, and friendly enough to call me Nicky now?"

Biting back an answering smile, she pumped down the chair and removed the cape. "It means I'd be a fool if I didn't boot you out and lock up my shop—Mr. Leclerc."

"You're a hard woman, Ms. Hudson." Laughing, he boosted himself out of the chair and walked to the front of the salon.

Lips parted and a hand pressed against her midriff, Carla watched his muscular body moving with animal grace under the buckskin shirt and jeans. To distract herself, she grabbed the broom and swept up a small mountain of black hair. When she bent over the dustpan, she could literally feel the heat of his dark eyes watching the pull of her breasts and hips against blouse and jeans. The raw sexual reaction blasting through her body was appalling.

Why?! she cried silently, tossing the broom back in the corner. Why should she be so attracted to this rover, this stranger passing in the night? She was pure and simply a homebody. It'd be insanity to give free rein to her desires.

Her knees felt like water when she walked to the desk. Avoiding his eyes, she looked down at her account books and bills. "This has been an interesting little interlude, but I really do have lots of work to do."

Nick pushed his hands into his jeans pockets. "I'll bet you haven't eaten yet. Want to have dinner with me?"

She glanced up, caught by the tinge of loneliness in his voice. As if that weren't difficult enough to resist, she imagined again that an eerie force was pushing them toward each other. She had to force herself to say the logical thing. "Thanks for asking, but I really can't."

He gazed at her with black eyes. "I can tell by your face that you feel it too. Something—I don't know what—something funny is going on between us. As if we were fated to meet. I'll bet we'd be wonderful together if you'd let yourself give in to it."

Heart leaping, she wrapped her arms around her body. It was too scary if he felt the pull too. "I don't care what's buzzing around us. You'll be rovin' on tomorrow, camera bum, and I don't do one-night stands."

He looked as if he might argue the point, but changed his mind. Lifting the rear of his buckskin shirt for his wallet, he said, "Then there's nothing left but to pay up. How much is the arm and leg you're charging?"

Money was the furthest thing from Carla's mind. She waved at the rock-bottom prices printed on a sign behind her desk. "Maybe double my regular cut fee for both hair and beard."

Nick shot her an almost panicked expression. Then he turned to scowl at the sign, worrying his upper lip with his bottom teeth.

Watching him curiously, she wondered if he was such a tightwad that he thought she was overcharging. Or was his tale of being a photographer a fabrication and he was low on cash? "A haircut and a half then. I'll call us even if you explain why you thought I should know Nick Leclerc."

"It's a deal." He turned away from the sign in obvious relief and filled out a check, slipping it between the pages of her account book. "That should explain everything," he said, walking toward the door.

Carla picked up his limp, feathered hat and held it out with two fingers. "I'd hate to find this lying in wait when I open up shop on Monday."

"Don't sneer at the poor thing—it's been trodden by horses." Nick put it on, tugged it around, then tucked it in his sash. "Doesn't fit without the hair."

"What a shame," she commiserated, eyes sparkling.

Opening the door, he still lingered. "Would you go out to dinner with me if we should happen to meet again?"

She gazed at him wistfully. "A Montanan like me isn't likely to run into a California camera bum like you more than once in a lifetime."

"Oh, I have a feeling fate'll throw us together again someday, somewhere." Twitching his brows up in a salute, he finally closed the door after himself.

Carla stood motionless for a moment, astonished by how empty and echoingly quiet the salon was now that he was gone. How lonely. At thirty, she'd had her fair share of romantic experiences, but she'd never felt so *bewitched* by a man before. He was correct in saying it felt as if they were meant to be. But that was impossible. They didn't have a thing in common.

An urge to finger something he'd touched induced her to take his check out of the account book. Her chin dropped when she saw the figure he'd written in: enough to bring the power bill for the ranch to its knees. She wouldn't have asked that much in her wildest dreams.

Then the logo at the top-left-hand corner hit her like a slap. WILDERNESS ENTERPRISES, INC.

A glance at the "Nicholas Leclerc" signed on the bottom cleared up the mystery of his name sounding vaguely familiar. The French pronunciation had

THE FOREVER MAN • 13

thrown her off, but an identical signature, big as life, was on a lease granting him six months' unrestricted rights to half the Hudson land.

What on *earth* did a man like Nick want with her great-aunt's run-down ranch? And why hadn't he told her right up front who he was? What was he hiding?

"Darn you, Auntie Grace," she muttered, throwing the check vexatiously on the account book. "What have you gotten me into?"

TWO

The next day was Sunday, a balmy June morning. After early church, Carla ran upstairs to her old girlhood room to change into a red tank top and short shorts. Back downstairs in the all-purpose country kitchen, she poured a cup of coffee and stood at the open window, too distracted to be aware of the early-summer scents and the trilling of birds.

Grace was sitting at the oak table, ready for late church in no-nonsense shoes, a vintage suit, and a hat clamped over flyaway white hair. "You're up awful early on your day off, aintcha?" she asked. "Something spurrin' you?"

"It sure is." Carla leaned her hips against the sill. "Wilderness Enterprises, Inc. turned up in my salon last night. Nicholas Leclerc, in person."

Grace eyed her niece with faded blue eyes. "Did he say what his intentions for Papa's place are?"

"No, and I don't trust him one bit."

"Why? What's wrong with 'im?"

Carla threw herself on a chair by the table and ran spread fingers through her hair. "Nothing. Everything! Top of the list: Why was he so secretive? Next is the fact that he's a photographer from Hollywood, of all places. I don't want any part of that jaded culture coming into my peaceful little community. It feeds on gullible people. I'll never forgive them for what they did to Janet."

Grace patted her hand. "I won't pretend to know how it felt to lose your sister to that miserable scandal. But I been knockin' around this old world for eighty years, and I do know you can't run away from hurts."

"That doesn't mean I'll welcome them into my backyard." Carla slammed her fist down on the table. "Dammit, I knew leasing the land to someone we didn't know would end up in disaster! I felt it in my bones."

Her aunt lifted her wattled chin defensively. "Well, it was *my* bones the vultures were chewin' at. I was about to lose Papa's place, and it ain't out of danger yet. The lease runs through hunting season, so this wildman is probably just an outfitter. We can live with that, can't we?"

"I suppose." Carla drummed her nails on the table, trying to picture Nick with a rifle in his hands.

"I better leave or I'll be late to church." Grace got up, slung a purse over her arm, and yanked the screen door open. A cattle dog, a mottled gray heeler, shot out from under the table, scrabbling across the waxed linoleum to whisk past her legs. "Pip, you fleabag dog," she bellowed, clumping down the steps of the back stoop. "I oughta hand you over to the cat-food factory."

Carla laughed, shaking her head. She adored the crusty old woman who had enveloped her and Janet in love and security for four years after their mother had died. She meant to reciprocate by making her aunt's last years secure. A difficult undertaking, Grace being Grace.

Refilling her cup, she sat down at the table to read the Sunday comics and to breakfast on cookies. After half an hour, she cocked her head to the sound of Pip barking, and to a good solid knock on the front door.

Tugging at her shorts, she walked down the central hall to the foyer. The door was open for fresh air, and she could make out the form of a man outside the screen. The dog was barking threateningly around his legs.

Apparently he could see her, too, because he asked, "Is this beast going to feast on my haunch or what?"

The very air around Carla caught its breath at the sound of Nick's voice. Her heart leaped with excitement and apprehension. "Lay down, Pip!" she said, subduing the dog. "Well, well, if it isn't Mr. Wilderness Enterprises himself."

"Well, well, if it isn't Ms. Hudson's Hair. See, I told you fate would step in and bring us together again."

"Oh, sure, fate," she said, squinting at him through the screen.

He squinted back with a grin that pressed creases into his cheeks and gave his ebony eyes a gleam. Then he scratched at the screen with curved fingers. "I feel like a prisoner greeting a visitor through a security barrier. Could I come inside?"

"I guess." She opened the door, shoving Pip back with an extended leg while Nick came in. "I thought you were flying back to California today," she said after she'd closed the door in the dog's face.

"You know, that's kind of funny," he said, rubbing the back of his neck. "I had every intention of going to the airport when I got on the Bitterroot Stage with my crew. But when we came to that big old white arch over your driveway, something seemed to call out to me to stay. I remembered some urgent business I wanted to take care of here, so I had the driver stop the bus and let me off."

The cookies turned heavy in Carla's stomach. "What kind of 'urgent business'?"

"I wondered if you'd have Sunday brunch with me, and whether you're ready to call me Nicky yet."

His voice was so cheeky, she couldn't help but laugh. He made a tempting sight with his hands slipped into his trouser pockets, his tan corduroy jacket pushed back from his chest, and a patch of black hair showing in the open neck of his white shirt, but she had to say, "The answer is no on both counts. The circumstances are too complicated. You know it, too, or you wouldn't have been pussyfooting around last night, instead of telling me who you were."

He winced. "Well, forget brunch then, that just came to me on the spur of the moment."

"Right, because it's time for you to answer some questions. Like why were you so determined to lease this particular ranch?"

"Because I'm interested in western history, and there's plenty of that here." The look on his face indicated it was only a fraction of the answer, but he turned away to look through the arch into the living room, at ornate woodwork, knickknacks and wall-hangings, furniture stiffly upholstered with thread-bare brocades and velvet. "Must be like living in a museum, living here."

"Maybe, but I love it." Carla slipped past him and pointed to a framed document on the inner wall. "If you're such a history buff, this letter should interest you. It was sent to my great-grandfather by Father Ravalli in the eighteen hundreds. He came to the Bitterroot Valley as a missionary to the Flathead Indians. Go ahead and read it."

A trapped expression hit Nick's face for a second before he stepped closer and scowled at the letter, biting into his upper lip.

Perching on a blue velvet wing chair, Carla watched him, wondering if he was nearsighted and too proud to wear glasses.

She covertly tried to pull her shorts down, but he

caught the motion as he turned away from the letter. Very slowly, his lips parted. He let his warm gaze move languorously over her shapely legs, then caress her body, and finally come to rest on her face. Sitting on the mate to her chair, he leaned forward, elbows on knees. "Can I ask you a question?"

Her breath seemed to have gotten all tangled up in her lungs, and every inch of her body felt as if it had been touched and sparked to tingling life. It surprised her that she could talk. "Sure, but I won't promise to answer."

His frown was perfectly serious. "What exactly is it that you don't like about me?"

The question took Carla by surprise, and she laughed. "I like you just fine, I think you're a kick."

He threw back his head in a laugh. "If I'm Nick the kick, then why are you vetoing me out? No dinner last night, no brunch today. All the barriers up."

Carla hitched forward on the chair. "Honestly, you make things so embarrassing. Most men back off at the first hint of a cold shoulder, but a woman has to club you over the head to get the message across."

"I just want to know why I'm getting clubbed, that's all." He hitched forward so their knees were almost touching. "There's some kind of funny chemistry going on between us, and it'd be a crying shame not to explore it."

Carla shook her head. "Maybe there is, maybe there isn't, but I'm no explorer. If I ever decide to get involved again, I want the whole package—home, kids, and a man who'll be with me forever." She lifted her chin and smiled sweetly at him. "There, camera bum, that should scare you off once and for all."

Nick smiled back just as sweetly. "I'm not so easily discouraged when I set my mind to something." After another thought, he went sober and studied her with eyes so dark, they seemed to pierce her soul. "But you're right, I wouldn't qualify as a forever man. So it's my lifestyle that puts you off then? Not the Enterprise?"

"The Enterprise . . . ? Oh, your outfit. Well, of course it puts me off, mainly because you still haven't told me what you intend to do with the ranch. Let me go on record by saying that Grace went against my wishes when she leased part of the ranch to you, sight unseen. I'm not as trusting and good-hearted as country people are."

"Acknowledged," Nick said, then jumped up as if he found it impossible to sit still for any length of time. "Why don't you show me what I've rented?"

"Lord, you are as slippery as an eel when it comes to explaining things! Oh, all right, the truth is bound to surface sooner or later."

Pip growled at Nick when they came out on the porch, but subsided and happily led the way when Carla ran down the steps and walked across the yard.

Her skin was prickled by an odd sense of anticipation quivering in the air. The world seemed more vivid because of it: cottonwoods in vigorous leaf, rugged mountains rearing granite heads against a brilliant blue sky, meadowlarks trilling on fence posts. Nick seemed to feel it, too, and glanced around, then pulled in a huge breath of crystal-clean air. "I didn't realize before how gorgeous a day it is."

"Yes, it is," she said, watching a ragged V of Canada geese come in for a splattering landing on a pond. "I may not earn as much money here in the valley, but do you have anything in Los Angeles to equal this?"

"At the moment, here's what I think of Los Angeles." He lifted his fists and jabbed both thumbs downward.

Interpreting this as a threat, Pip rushed back with bared fangs to rescue Carla. He yelped when she tripped over him. "Pip, for Pete's sake!" she cried out, flailing her arms for balance.

Nick caught her by the shoulders, then circled his arms around her waist, smiling down at her. "Maybe that bloodthirsty beast has some merits after all."

Wrapped in his spicy male scent, she held her arms against her sides, resisting an urge to curve herself into his body, unable to control a throaty little laugh. "Did you sneak in last night and work out a system of hand signals with him?"

"Me? Nah-h-h, never." Nick kissed the upturned tip of her nose. "I swear my motives are lily-white and innocent."

"You're about as innocent as Attila the Hun," she declared, reluctantly pulling free of his arms.

Nick threw back his head in that captivating laugh of his, and turned to look at the outbuildings: bunkhouse, hay barns, stables, and corrals. Everything badly needed paint, starting with the driveway arch emblazoned with the name Hudson and the pierced *H* brand, right down to a dilapidated one-story house that had captured his interest. "What's this place?" he asked, cupping his hands around his eyes to look in a dirty window.

"The jockey house," she said, trying to straighten a shutter hanging on one hinge. It came off in her hands. "My great-grandfather got rich mining gold around the turn of the century, but horse racing was his passion. He kept a jockey on salary until he'd gambled everything away. Grace is still paying off good old Papa's debts."

He nodded. "Any chance of me using this for a home away from home for the duration of the lease?"

Carla stared at him, then glanced at the ranch house. She'd never get any sleep with this man in plain sight of her bedroom. "You don't want to live here," she said, shaking her head until her short hair swirled around her face. "It's in terrible shape—no furniture, no appliances. And too far from the land we leased you."

"Mmmm . . ." he responded, lifting his scarred left brow. "Where is my land?"

Carla waved a hand toward the west, where the ranch butted up against the Bitterroots and pine forests flowed out of a great gash of a canyon. "From that bluff over there, to the crag."

An eager, excited expression lit his face. "Can we walk out there?"

"Sure, I guess." She opened a gate in a rail fence and they passed through into a pasture. "You still haven't told me why you were so anxious to lease land you've never seen," she said.

"Oh, I've seen your ranch before, I just didn't know which hundred acres I got. Bunny threshed out the contract."

"Bunny?" Carla repeated, recalling that Bunny had come up in the conversation the night before.

"I expect she used her legal name, Bernice Fletcher. Bunny tends the business end of the Enterprise for me."

Glancing at him, she asked, "What *is* Wilderness Enterprises, exactly?"

"My base for photographic operations in LA."

"Why are you moving it here?"

"I'm not. It's only temporary, to . . . for a special project."

A herd of a dozen horses interrupted to nuzzle Carla and snort at Nick's unfamiliar scent. He rubbed necks and ears. "As these big babies Hudson horses?"

"Only this one," she said, running a hand over the silky flank of Molly, a pretty little black. "We take in boarders for extra income."

"You must be busy, helping run a ranch on top of your hair shop."

"Maybe, but I don't mind. I'd do anything for Grace."

He glanced at her, his eyes soft. "Amazing Grace?"

"You'll find out how amazing when you tangle with her a time or two. Anyhow, the only other help she can afford is a handyman, Lester, and he's even older and stiffer than she is." Carla smiled. "They've been sweet on each other since childhood. I don't know why she didn't marry him."

He grinned. "Because she's probably as hard to pin down as you are. The trait runs in the family, no doubt."

"Keep it up, buddy," she warned, laughing. "I might decide to break your lease."

Nick lifted his dimpled chin. "I have no doubt Bunny tied this land up so tight, nothing can get you out of the rental agreement. Short of maybe selling me your body."

"In your dreams, camera bum," she said, embarrassed that her voice sounded husky and breathless. "You couldn't begin to afford my body."

Spinning away to hide a blush, she followed an urge pulling her toward the mountains.

Nick followed Carla as if drawn by a siren song. She had a Mother Nature sort of beauty that fit into the great outdoors. Fit his style. In fact, he liked her too damn much for his own good. She was everything he might have dreamed of in a woman, if he'd been forever material. Sexy as hell, smart enough to run a business, witty, and pert. It tickled him to have her sass him right back.

A randy smile crept over his face as he watched the motion of her body climbing up an outcropping of rocks at the base of the mountain. His lips itched to kiss the graceful neck curving down from her short hair. And what he wouldn't give to fill his hands with the rounded cheeks undulating under her white shorts.

She nipped off his fantasy at the top of the promontory by announcing, "Your land starts here."

The oddest sensation came over him when he stood on the brink of the ridge looking out over the valley. It was as if he'd come home to something left unfinished or in need of resolution. He could almost hear a whisper of welcome in the boughs of the ponderosa pines. The feeling melded with the urge he'd had a couple of years earlier when he'd turned thirty: the need to be tied to something. Urges like that put a ramblin' man in a downright vulnerable position, so he hoped they'd pass once he explored them.

"My sister and I used to come here when we were kids," Carla said, sitting down on a sun-warmed boulder. "We used to pretend we were princesses, with all the valley spread out below for our kingdom."

Nick braced a boot on the boulder and looked down at her. "Lucky you to have a sister; I was a lonely only."

She glanced up at him, then away. "I am, too, now. She died about three years ago."

"Sorry," he said softly, wincing over his gaffe, and veered to a safer subject. "What kind of a kid were you?"

"A tomboy—galloping on horses, hiking, falling in the river, tormenting Grace. At least while I lived here, from the time I was eight to twelve years old." She grinned at him. "I suppose you were a perfectly cherubic little boy."

"Me, a cherub?" Lowering himself to the ground, he leaned his back against the boulder, close enough to her legs to catch a whiff of her perfume. He ached to touch her, to do a hell of a lot more than touch, but she seemed too special to push his luck. He gave a short laugh. "I was the kind of kid it's a wonder someone didn't tie in a sack and throw in the river."

"Somehow that doesn't surprise me." Carla smiled, and touched a finger to his left brow. "How'd you get the scar?"

He covered her small hand with his big one, holding the touch against his forehead. She pulled away too quickly for his taste. "Battle scars from my perpetual war against whichever private school I happened to be in at the time. At age eleven I tried to escape in the night by sneaking down a trellis, which promptly ripped off the building." He glanced up at her, laughing. "I fell down on my head and went boom."

Sympathy softened her face when she sensed how lonely he'd felt. "You must have minded terribly not having a normal home life. If there is such a thing."

Nick had always been phobic about sympathy, and cursed himself for bringing up the topic of childhood. "Yes, I minded being railroaded to boarding school," he said curtly. "But I loved spending my summers traveling with my granddad. He taught me to love the wild, and do things like chase after those damned Amazon Indians that won't let me track them down. I wouldn't have spent my last two months fighting my way up the Salmon River if it weren't for him."

He lifted his head and grinned. "You know what they call the Salmon, don't you? Do you think it's significant that I came to you on the *River of No Return?*"

"I'd be a fool to bite on that bait," she said.

Heaving a sigh, he stretched himself out full-length on the gravelly, sparsely grassed ground, his jacket rolled up and jammed under his head. He felt lazy as a cat with the sun beaming down on him. Carla was glancing sidelong at his body, and it excited him to know she was attracted. He circled his fingers around her wrist and tugged. "Come on down and make yourself comfortable. You're too far away."

She resisted only a moment, then shifted off the boulder to sit with her bare legs stretched out beside him, her tank top a red splash against the gray granite. "This is so-o-o nice," he murmured, turning on his side to face her.

"Mmmm, but risky without a chaperon, I think." She whistled for Pip, snapping her fingers. The dog tore out of the trees and insinuated himself between them, raising his lip and rumbling at Nick.

"Chicken," Nick murmured, hoping the beast's attitude was mostly show.

"Not chicken, smart. My Aunt Grace didn't bring up any fools," Carla said, ruffling the thick fur on Pip's neck. "Okay, time to quit stalling—why did you rent the ranch?"

He'd been putting off the answer because he suspected she wouldn't like it. "I'll start at the beginning so you can see the total picture. See, my great-great-grandfather, Pierre Leclerc, was a fur trapper. He kept a journal about everything he did. My grandfather read it to me, so I know Pierre came to the Bitterroot Valley, married a Flathead Indian woman, and had several children. His oldest son, Michel, went back to France and had a family, including my granddad."

"Very interesting, but—" Carla began, then bit back a yawn and leaned her head sleepily against the boulder, long, thick lashes spreading over her cheeks.

Nick hoped his story would go over better now that she was bored and sleepy. "When Granddad retired, we began following old Pierre's trapping trail as it was described in his journal. The Salmon was the last leg of our odyssey." He paused, then added cautiously, "The trail ends here."

After a second, Carla slitted her eyes open. "Here in Montana . . . ?"

He patted the ground, eliciting a grumble from the dog. "Here on your ranch."

"Here!" She brought her head upright.

"Uh-huh. Pierre staked out an acreage, but your . . . ah . . . one of the settlers ousted him and his family along with the Indians when the government relocated the Flathead tribe onto the reservation up north. Stole his land."

"Spit it out—what exactly are you trying to say?" Carla asked angrily.

Nick dug under his back and took out a stone, tossed it up and caught it. He hated antagonizing her, but Pierre's story had always been so important a part of his life; at this point, it was his top priority. "By all rights, this ranch belongs in Leclerc hands."

Sparks sputtered in her eyes. "My ancestors did not steal this place. The first Hudson came from Ohio and grubbed the ranch out with honest sweat."

He tossed the stone up. "Are you positive about that?"

Carla nodded vigorously, then said. "Yes-s-s."

"Pierre's ranch is described in his journal, down to the shape of the mountains and other landmarks. He even wrote about this exact spot. I intend to look for the site where he built a log cabin. When I find the remains, I'll have proof." The idea sounded good, but he didn't really believe there'd be anything left of it after a hundred years.

Carla sat upright, her spine stiff as a poker. "If you rented the ranch for a fool's errand like proving you have some legal right to it, then you're wasting your time! I won't allow you to take Grace's home away from her."

"Oh, hell, I don't intend to take anything away from anyone. What wold I do with a ranch?"

"Well, what *do* you want then?"

Nick hunched up on an elbow, ignoring Pip's warning fangs. "I believe it's vitally important to expose the bigotry of the past, because the same thing is going on yet. The unwanted *still* seldom get a say in what happens to them. The best way to educate people and change the world is by wringing a few hearts with a strong story and powerful characterizations. That's why I wrote the screenplay."

"*What* screenplay?"

"The one I told you about last night. Preston Mann

and I are making a movie about your"—he broke off and cleared his throat—"about the settler ousting Pierre for his connection with the Indians."

Her face was a map of bewilderment. "Your script is going to be *produced*?!"

Nick sat up and wrapped his arms around his knees, excitement stirring his heart all over again. "Uh-huh. I had to hog-tie Pres down to get him to read it, but he liked it and agreed to be the producer/ director. Bunny's in on it, too, a big plus since she's a genius. We're working on a shoestring, but by gosh, we're going to do it!" A smile lit his face. "The film is the climax of my lifelong dream."

Carla ran horrified fingers through her short hair, leaving it in wild disarray. "You're going to film a *movie* on Grace's ranch?"

"We all agreed it'd have more impact if the location was authentic." Nick swept his hand in an arc, encompassing the mountains on both sides of the valley, the river winding down the middle. "Can't you see how beautiful this'll be on film?"

She wouldn't even look. "No one would pay money to watch an *oater*. Two men fighting over a ranch has been done a zillion times."

"It's not an oater, and it isn't about the ranch! It's about a love affair between Pierre's son, Michel, and the settler's daughter, Emily. They—"

Nick broke off when he heard a soft "aahhh." He glanced toward the pines, and realized Carla was looking too. Good God, he thought, they hadn't both heard a voice that wasn't there, had they?

Shaken, he resumed his spiel. "It was acceptable for trappers and settlers to cavort with Indian women, but they frowned upon the products of those relationships nosing around their daughters. *That's* why Pierre and his family were booted out. To break up a love affair between Emily and Michel. See?"

"Nick Leclerc, my social conscience is just as well

developed as yours!" Carla said in a controlled voice. "But surely you don't expect me to stamp an okay on your using Grace's ranch to make a movie about her grandfather being a *dishonest bigot!*"

He hadn't thought of it from that aspect. "But, Carla, the incident took place a hundred years ago. And we aren't going to use real names in the movie."

"You don't know Grace—she'd guess, and as far as she's concerned, her ancestors are all saints." Carla threw her arms out. "How am I supposed to explain something like this to her? At her age she'd probably have a stroke!"

"Now you know why I put off telling you," Nick said, hunching his shoulders. "As soon as I talked to you last night I knew you wouldn't take kindly to my little project."

"I certainly don't."

He threw the stone over the edge of the ridge. "With your background in films I hope you realize it's too late to call it off, even if I wanted to. Megabucks have gone down. The cast has been selected and rehearsed. The crews and materials are on board. Preston is shooting the close-ups and interiors back in Los Angeles."

Carla got up on her feet and jerked her red tank top down over her breasts. "Nick, you cannot waltz onto my ranch and do this. I won't allow it!"

He hoisted himself up on his feet, wishing there was a simple way out. "You didn't write any restrictions into the fine print of the lease, so—"

"You can damn well be sure I would have, if I'd had any say in it! Darn that Grace!"

"You didn't, she didn't, no one did. The rent is paid up through November, so we *are* going to make that movie here." He raised his brows and scratched a cheek. "It won't be so awful, trust me."

"*Trust you!*" Carla stared at him; her mouth worked,

but no additional words came out. Spinning around, she began descending the ridge of rocks.

Nick grabbed his jacket and followed, wishing all they had to think about was the attraction that might have blossomed between them. A big fat nothing was going to come of it if she insisted on setting off a cowboy-Indian war.

Crossing the pasture, they formed a parade of sorts, Pip in the lead, Nick following Carla, and a dozen horses bringing up the rear, single file. Everything came to a halt when she spun around. "Grace may have let you get a toehold," she announced. "But that won't stop her from taking a shotgun to you if you play free and easy with Hudson honor and her papa's ranch."

He made the mistake of laughing over the image, but rubbed the grin off his face when she scowled. "Then I better charm Amazing Grace over to my side, hadn't I?"

"Oh, right, I forgot. You're an expert in the charm department, aren't you?" Her eyes flashed angrily. "You came into my salon last night thinking you could charm me into accepting that miserable movie, didn't you?"

"You saw the way I looked—I *did* need a haircut. Maybe I was a little curious about you, too, but . . ." Carla's expression told Nick he was painting himself ever deeper into a corner. He sighed. "I suppose this means you won't be calling me Nicky anytime in the near future?"

To his enormous relief, she bit her lip to check a grin, then lost the struggle and laughed. "You are the most *utterly* incorrigible man I've ever met!"

"Oh, thank you, God, she's smiling. Maybe there's hope after all!"

"Don't count on it. In fact, I might break out that shotgun myself." Carla turned her back and began marching again.

When they reached the circle drive in front of the house, she suggested pointedly, "I'm sure you have somewhere to go."

Nick had been in the wilderness so long, he had a million urgent business odds and ends to take care of back in LA. He could, and should, call a taxi and go arrange for another flight; instead he tried to prolong his time with this lovely, furious woman. "I can't go very far without transportation."

"Now you expert me to chauffeur you around?"

"You'd get rid of me sooner if you gave me a ride to Missoula for a flight out," he suggested hopefully, knowing it meant an hour alone with her in a car.

"I don't suppose I can argue that," she said. "Come on, then."

Far from wanting to be rid of Nick, Carla felt a bottomless sense of emptiness when she stopped her car in front of the airport terminal. She didn't want him to leave, but it was ridiculous to pine after . . . well . . . the enemy. "I suppose like a bad penny you're bound to turn up again?"

He pulled up a knee, in no hurry to get out of the car. "I'm afraid so. I've invested my entire life savings in this movie project, so I intend to be right here as a technical adviser to see it's done right. I'll be back before the filming begins, and that should be around the end of August."

Carla turned sideways, bracing her arm over the top of the steering wheel, and studied him for a moment. "Nick, I'm going to be very honest with you. I don't want any Hollywood people coming into the valley. And I intend to do everything in my power to break your lease. Or at least to prohibit the movie from being made on our ranch."

"I'm sorry you feel that way." Tiny muscles in his jaw knotted. "Making this movie is important to me, and I intend to go through with it. I don't think you can stop me."

"We'll see."

"Oh, dammit, I don't want to fight with you!" Nick turned to face her. "Lord, I wish we'd met some other time, some other place, without all this hassle to thresh out."

"Yes, I wish we had, too, Nick," she said, amazed to feel her lips trembling.

"Do you really? I'm glad." Eyes dark and hot, he leaned forward and took her face between his hands. "You're such a lovely, alive woman, Carla," he whispered, brushing his lips against her mouth. "I've been aching to touch you ever since I walked into your shop."

Going weak with the scent and heat of him, she melted into his warm kiss. When he touched his tongue to her lip, the sensation spread through her body, centering at her core. She pulled her mouth away, frightened of the urgent sexual desire she felt for this man who was so wrong for her.

Drawing a deep, tremulous breath, Nick gazed at her with a puzzled, almost stunned expression, as if the kiss had shocked him too. He touched her hair, then her face, gently, as a blind man might explore, then dropped his hands onto his knees and gave a crooked smile. "Well, how about that?"

"Yes, how about that?" she whispered, just as stunned. "I think you've had lots of experience in good-bye kisses, camera bum."

"That wasn't a good-bye, it was a sample. When I come back, we're going to explore this thing going on between us."

Carla's heart leaped in anticipation, but she firmly shook her head.

Nick just as firmly nodded, and grazed his fingertips down the curve of her long, slender neck. Then he got out of the car and walked away. Carla cupped a hand around her tingling neck and watched him disappear into the terminal. She felt as if her life were being drawn away with him.

It might take every single minute of the two months he'd be gone to build an immunity to him, she suspected. But build it she would, because she had a war to wage.

Three

"It's August already!" Carla lamented, jabbing a french fry in ketchup. "I've been fighting this war for over two months, and no one is paying any attention to me! My lawyer can't find any loopholes in the lease. No one would sign a petition against the movie. The city council hopes the valley might become a sort of summer-camp Hollywood."

She and her married friends had gathered for girls' night out in a back booth of the Coffee Cup, a folksy cafe with a plethora of antiques displayed on shelves under the ceiling. She looked imploringly at each young woman. "Can't anyone think of a way to prevent the filming?"

Bonnie, a real estate agent, poked at her salad. "I'm having trouble sympathizing. Business is boomin'. Movie people have snapped up every rental within ten miles."

"That's what I mean. Trailers, semis, and RVs are popping up like toadstools on Grace's ranch too. Don't you realize that turning a band of kinky people loose on this rural community is like setting a pack of coyotes free in a herd of lambs? They'll run roughshod all over us!"

Gayle talked around a bite of burger. "Come on, be

fair. Their blurbs in the *Ravalli Republic* indicate
they're making every effort to consider the wishes of
the community."

Jill, one of Carla's hairstylists, piped up, "And
they're makin' jobs. Even my Ralph is workin' again."

Carla had to back down, knowing how tough the
young woman had it, supporting herself and her
charmer of a husband on the pittance she earned at
the salon. "Let's change the subject," she said.

"We've heard suspiciously little about this Nick
Leclerc," Bonnie said. "What's he like?"

Nick wasn't the subject Carla would have chosen.
Her immunity had gone even worse than her war,
and she alternated between dreading and aching for
his return. "Oh, you know, you've seen one man,
you've seen 'em all."

A chorus of "Oo-o-h-hs" went up. "Come on, you
can't fool us."

Gayle dabbed her lips with a napkin. "I dumped on
you when I agonized over falling in love with Cass
last year. Now I'm standing by, ready to return the
favor."

Carla shoved her sweaty palms into the pockets of
her western jeans. "Sorry to disappoint you—"

Bonnie grinned. "Sure, we've all been there."

"—but I am not interested in Nick."

"Then why is your face so rosy red?" Jill asked
slyly.

Carla gave in and tossed out the understatement
of the century. "Maybe there's a slight attraction."

"Uh-*huh*!" Gayle nodded. "What's he look like?"

"I don't know—black-haired, black-eyed, brassy,
and bold, I guess." Carla crossed her knees and
jiggled her booted foot. "I really do envy the three of
you, married to your special men. I'd give anything to
find a guy meant just for me, but I'm too mouthy and
opinionated for the country men around here. Then
when I find someone who appeals to me, he's a

camera bum, and won't stick around long enough to build a dream. And that's the whole story."

"How sad and unfair," Jill said. "Couldn't you have a little affair?"

Carla shook her head. "I might have a decade ago, back in another era. Luckily, I've picked up enough common sense and maturity along the way not to jump pell-mell into wild excitement anymore."

Gayle grinned. "Look at you, tempting fate with those noble words."

Fate again. "He'll be living way across the ranch in the RVs, and he'll leave in November when his lease is up. I certainly ought to be able to control myself for three months." She wiped her mouth, crushed the napkin into a ball, and got up. "Time to go home."

It was fully dark by the time Carla got out of her car. Pip rushed up, yelping and jumping as she climbed the steps of the back stoop. At the door, she frowned over a tremor of odd excitement in the atmosphere, calling out, welcoming her home. Puzzled, she turned and looked out over the ranch.

Ruddy flames were dancing near the outbuildings. "*Fire!*" she cried out.

Tearing the door open, she rushed into the kitchen, Pip nipping her heels. "There's a fire at the bunkhouse!"

Lester was sitting at the table. Grace calmly put a platter of pot roast on the table and sat down. "Ain't no fire fire, it's a camp fire. That young wildman came back today. Asked all prissy polite, would it be all right if he used the jockey house. I gave him the go-ahead."

"You *didn't!*" Carla groaned.

"I told him it was run-down, but he says he don't mind roughin' it and cookin' out on a camp fire until he gets it fixed up, so I says—"

"Damn! Damn, damn," Carla whispered. How could

she resist the man if he was parked right in her backyard?

"Since he's a guest on our place, so to speak," her aunt said, a puckish expression on her wrinkled face, "why don't you go ask 'im to have supper with us? We got plenty."

"Oh, now you're throwing good old country hospitality up to me!" Carla twisted her lips in a self-mocking smile, knowing she'd been aching for an excuse to go see Nick. She got up and marched toward the door. "I suppose I'll have to go ask him then, seeing as you're the boss."

"My bein' the boss never cut any ice with her before," Grace said to Lester, then held up a hand. "Oh, by the way, the feller said to tell Carla Nicky's back. Stressed 'Nicky.' Does that mean somethin'?"

"No, it does not!" Carla snapped, jerking the screen door open with a squawk of the spring. Pip whisked past, almost tripping her as she ran down the steps.

A gentle night breeze had blown away the August day heat and stirred up the mellow ranch scents. On it were murmurs, beckoning her forward. She walked down the familiar path, lit only by the faint light of the high half-moon and the glittering of billions of stars.

The fire was much smaller than Carla had thought, situated safely away from the buildings. A black sport wagon was parked near it, tailgate down. She stopped, hidden by darkness, and gazed at Nick.

In boots, jeans, and a white shirt rolled up at the sleeves, he was sitting on a chunk of wood with his feet tucked back, knees jutting, as big and broad-shouldered as she remembered. When he poked a stick at a burning log, a flock of sparks exploded up into the black sky: a pretty fair reflection of her reaction to him. Flame light danced on his face, giving him a primitive look when he glanced in her direction. "Do you like what you see?"

"How'd you know I was here?" It was so dark, she could barely see Pip right next to her.

A grin spread over his face. "The breeze told me you were coming, and when you came near, vibrations and feelers reached out to me."

She stared at him, wondering if there actually was something in the air. Then she glanced back at the house, lit by a yard light. "You saw me come out and head in this direction."

"That too," he admitted. "Want to come in out of the dark?"

Carla walked forward as Pip commented with rumbling growls about the trespasser.

"Brought your bodyguard, I see," Nick said.

She wrapped a hand around the heeler's muzzle, shutting him up. "Would that I could peel myself away from him."

Folding her legs, she sat down on the grassy ground, a safe distance separating her from temptation. The breeze puffed a cloud of smoke her way, forcing her to get up, circle the fire, and sit far too close. Nick's smiling, inviting gaze blanketed her, caressing the most sensitive areas of her body.

Silence seemed to stretch eternally; to break it she blurted out the first thing that came to mind: "Your hair looks shaggy—haven't you had it cut since you left here?"

He ran his fingers through waves that fell over his ears and curls that reached his shoulders in back. "Of course I haven't. I'm not promiscuous—I wouldn't cheat on my hairstylist. I've never had a more stirring . . . uh . . . encounter than we had that evening." The cocky smile she remembered so well flashed white in the firelight. "Was it good for you too?"

"All I remember is your sassy mouth," she shot back, cursing herself for bringing up something that had fed her fantasies for two months. "When did you get here?"

"This afternoon, and I've been waiting for you ever since. In fact, I've been waiting two months. You're the damnedest woman to interfere with a man's concentration." He poked the log again, sending sparks flaring, then glanced up at her. "Did you miss me too?"

She clasped her arms around her knees and smiled back at him. "You crossed my mind now and again, but don't let it go to your head. I only came out here because Grace told me to tell you you're welcome to eat supper with her and Lester. They're having pot roast and mashed potatoes."

The breeze shifted, so smoke forced her a few feet closer to him. His black eyes were hot, caressing her face with an invitation. "You sure you didn't come because you're ready to call me Nicky?"

"Absolutely." Before some rather primitive desires could crumble her adamant denial, Carla unfolded her legs and started to get up. "I've extended the country hospitality, so I'd better go back to the house. If you want supper, come along."

He reached out and captured her hand, stopping her. "Don't go, please. Can't we talk for a while? Let's see, what shall we talk about?" He shrugged. "I've had my dinner already—shish kebab."

As she stared at him, waves of sensation radiated from contact with his hand, running through her body like fire. "Shish kebab . . . ?" she repeated inanely, pulling free.

Nick held up the stick he'd been poking at the log, a long-handled skewer, then picked up a plastic plate with a few fire-grilled beef chunks and veggies. "Want some? I've got a bunch marinating yet— simple to roast another batch."

Food seemed a safe topic; Carla sat down, hitching farther away and positioning Pip between them. "Thanks, but no, I had french fries at the Coffee Cup."

"That's it? Fries?"

Picking up the skewer, she took over the job of poking at the log. "So I'm a junk-food freak; it's a free country."

"What you need is someone to educate you in nutrition."

"Is that what I need?"

"Among other things."

Nick laughed softly and glanced down at Pip, who had his unblinking eyes fixed upon the plate of scraps. "So it takes food to win you over, does it, beast?" He held out a morsel of meat, and Pip snapped it up. "Dammit, dog, the fingers weren't included!"

Carla laughed. "I could have warned you."

"Well, why didn't you?"

"Experience is the best teacher."

"Why do you keep this bloodthirsty creature around, anyhow?"

She put an arm around Pip and nuzzled the black patch covering the top half of his head. "He grows on you."

"*You've* grown on me." Nick leaned closer and reached over the dog to curl his hand around Carla's neck, running his fingers up into her hair. "I love this sassy little hairdo of yours. It'd be a sin to cover your neck. That's what I thought about most while we were apart—kissing your neck."

She stared into his dark eyes, imagining those kisses. Her skin was already tingling with a seductive, magical fantasy of his lips on her. Dangerously close to surrender, she pulled free and glanced toward the ramshackle house behind them. "I don't think it's going to work out for you to stay in the jockey house, Nick. It's a shambles and full of . . . *mouse droppings.*"

"Your concern is ever so touching." His eyes were full of fire and laughter. "Not to worry; until I get the mouse droppings swept out and some furniture brought in, I'll sleep on the porch . . . under the stars . . . in my sleeping bag."

The way he said it sounded like an invitation. Carla laced her arms across her midriff and forced herself to shake her head. "No, I want you to get an RV and settle on your leased land, over there in"—she wrinkled her nose—"Little Hollywood."

He leaned his dimpled chin on a fist and gazed at her with intense, challenging attention. "Why? Are you worried I'll be too close for comfort?"

She gave a shaky laugh. "You better believe that's what I think. I won't feel safe until you're way out there on the far end of the ranch."

"But I want to be right here, close," he said softly. "We've got some exploring to do, remember?"

"I never agreed to any such thing. The jockey house isn't included in your lease."

"But Amazing Grace is the one who signed the lease, and she said it was okay for me to live here."

Her mind wasn't functioning well enough for her to hold her own in a debate. "Oh, it's useless to argue with you. Do what you want. I've got to go." She pulled herself up onto her knees in a move toward rising, but didn't follow through. "If you insist upon roughing it, I suppose you can come up to the house and use the bathroom and whatnot."

"How gracious of you. One never knows when one might need a whatnot." He watched her, smiling knowingly. "But I wouldn't want to make a nuisance of myself."

Carla sat down again and laughed wryly. "*You* don't want to make a nuisance of yourself! May I direct your attention to Little Hollywood, over there at the base of the mountains? If that isn't a nuisance, what is? All that's missing are spotlights wagging back and forth across the sky."

The fire was burning down; Nick stood up and added the log he'd been sitting on, sending sparks flying wildly into the air. Then he folded himself onto the ground, closer to her, eliciting a series of growls from Pip. "I take it you're a little peeved over losing the war against my project."

"Not a little, a lot." She made a face. "I was a voice crying out in the wilderness—pun intended. Everyone thinks your damn movie is the greatest thing since John Owen built his trading post." She fingered Pip's velvety ears. "When is the shoot supposed to begin?"

"Hopefully, end of the month, but the last-minute details are killers," he said, then smiled. "They'll hold auditions for local extras in a couple of weeks. You ought to try out. Seems as if we should have a token Hudson in this particular movie."

"Ha-ha, very funny." The smoke tried to drive Carla closer to Nick again, but she got up on her knees instead in another well-intentioned move toward leaving. "I'm having enough trouble telling Grace that the plot is uncomplimentary to her family, without appearing in it myself. I suppose I'd better tell her before she hears it via neighborhood gossip."

Nick got up on his knees, too, facing her. "I met that formidable old lady today, and she seems clearheaded enough to accept what's going on. Aren't you underestimating her?"

Carla laughed shortly. "She said you were acting 'prissy polite,' trying to make an impression. I imagine she was reciprocating. So what do you know about anything?"

"Nothing. I'm just trying to pick my way through a touchy situation." Reaching out over the dog, he offered his hand, palm up. "If I've stepped on a sore nerve, I apologize."

Carla looked at the palm, then at his face. He was trying to look contrite, but laughter was below the surface—a fair alert that it wasn't safe to take his hand. "You've been stomping all over a whole network of screaming nerves," she said grumpily.

Smoke billowed at her again. "Why is this stuff following me, and not you?"

"I live a charmed life," Nick said smugly, reaching his hand out a little farther. "Tell you what—accept my apology, and I'll turn on my infamous charm and help you smooth the way with Amazing Grace."

"Infamous is right," Carla muttered.

Then, struck by a weak moment, she put her hand in his. The move was a serious mistake, because he used it to pull her closer to him, bending over Pip. Curling his other hand around the back of her neck, he covered her mouth with an urgent kiss, tugging at her lips, his tongue forcing entry.

She could no more have stopped herself from melting against him than levitate. The length of his body pressing against hers sent sensations crackling through her system. Needs she'd tried to bury flashed to life. The ferocity of her response frightened her into pulling away.

Only then her gaze became trapped in his midnight-black eyes. Bathed by their heat and the age-old question, every fiber of her body begged her to answer yes. She managed to shake her head. "Nick, stop, I don't want this."

"Yes you do, sweetheart. I can feel the very beat of your heart crying out for me. It's thrumming through the air, all around us. Feel it? You can tell how I'm starving for you, can't you?"

Oh yes, and she was starving too. "Nick. . . ."

Circling his arms around, he crushed her against his urgent body. He buried his face in the side of her neck and moved his lips against the long curve. "Carla, sweetheart, this is so much better than I dreamed it could be. Do you like it?"

"Yes . . . oh. . . ." She threw back her head to give his lips full possession of her neck, then pressed herself closer. Wanting him, her body on fire, she moaned low in her throat.

Lifting his head, he smiled down at the passion in

her face. "Let me show you I can be more than a nuisance."

Carla stared at him, her heart beating so rapidly she felt dizzy, her voice so breathless she could barely speak. "A nuisance . . . ? You're a veritable menace!"

He laughed softly, fluttering little kisses all around her face. "You're right, I am. So you might as well give up the battle, love, because sooner or later you're going to surrender and have me. It's fated."

If he'd said anything else, she might have given in that very moment, but fate frightened her. And fear activated a small remaining core of sanity in her mind. Pulling away, she shook her head slowly. "This isn't fate, it's hormones," she said in a raspy whisper. "And I am definitely leaving now."

His hands were shaking when he dropped them away from her. He rubbed his face and took a deep breath, then looked at her with bottomless dark eyes. "All right, run away back to the damn house, but I bet I know what you'll be thinking about all night in your lonely bed."

"This is all your fault," she muttered to Pip, lying between the two humans, his furry face puzzled. He'd allowed the kiss with nary a growl to protect his mistress from her own foolishness. "Some body-guard you are."

Climbing clumsily up on shaky legs, Carla walked to the far edge of the circle of firelight, the gentle breeze moaning around her, tugging her back. She paused, then stopped and looked back at Nick. "I won't make any more fuss about the movie, and you can even live in the jockey house if you want to. But what happened here tonight had better never happen again!"

He poked at the fire, sending a meteor shower of sparks up into the black sky. "You're talking about a long, hot, frustrating Indian summer, sweetheart."

Carla escaped into the darkness, tugged and tormented by the breeze.

Forget control, she told herself, running up onto the back stoop of the ranch house. Forget wisdom, maturity, and resistance. If she intended to come through Indian summer with her heart in one piece, she had to stay as far away from Nick Leclerc as humanly possible.

Four
_____

Carla parked her car in downtown Hamilton and
walked around to open the passenger door. "I don't
know how I let you drag me out of my salon to go to
these damn auditions."

Grace hitched herself arthritically to the edge of
the bucket seat. "Well, how could I have got here by
myself with all this material hangin' off me?"

Carla gathered the unwieldy train into her arms,
and helped Grace totter to her feet, shaking out her
bustled, jet-beaded, dark green dress. "Think they
might choose me as a movie extra?" she asked,
holding out her arms.

Her aunt had heard from gossip that the movie
would be based on local history; Carla knew she
should explain before things went any further, but
how could she, faced with Grace's excited eyes? "I
couldn't say," she said, brushing at her own blue
tailored blouse and divided skirt. "All I know is that
I feel like a sparrow beside a peacock."

"Well, you could've put on an outfit from the attic
and auditioned, too, if you weren't so scared you
might run into Nick Leclerc." Grace reached into the
backseat for a hat decorated with ribbons and bird
wings. "You been sneakin' around almost two weeks

avoidin' him. I don't know why you're so scared to take a chance."

Carla walked grumpily down the sidewalk by her aunt's side. "I don't see that you took any chances on Lester, sixty years ago."

"That was entirely different," Grace snapped. "You could have at least been at the ranch when that Bunny rabbit and Preston whatzisname came to introduce themselves. The director feller claims he knows you. Common decency oughta have spurred you to welcome old acquaintances to our place."

"Oh, now we're back to good old country hospitality, are we?" Carla murmured. "Too bad so much city rubbed off on me while I was away."

The film company's casting director had set up public relations headquarters in a rustic, arty mall with several shops spread along an inside arcade. Grace joined a group of other hopefuls sitting on folding chairs outside a shop with whited-out windows. They disappeared one by one as they were called to be auditioned, and when Grace's turn came, she swept in like a dowager queen.

Carla followed in her wake and stood by the door, looking around with more curiosity and interest than she cared to admit.

Spotlights were aimed at a table where the PR people were conducting the interviews. A bored cameraman with one dangling earring was shooting the proceedings. Several people lounging near the far wall were identifiable as film crew members by their quixotic clothing. The young woman in charge rose to her feet and gave Grace a 100-watt smile. "Hi, remember me? Bunny Fletcher. Come and sit down, we'll have a nice little chat."

Half-blinded by the bright lights, Carla tiptoed toward the darkened rear of the room. She gave a start and groaned inwardly when she reached the back corner. Nick was perched on a stool, tipped back with his shoulders braced against the wall, heels hooked on the lower rung, knees jutting: a man with a nerve-racking talent for falling into naturally seductive poses. "Hi," he whispered, his face alight with a challenging smile.

"Hi." Hitching herself up on a stool, she fussily arranged her blue culottes around her knees, trying to dampen her errant responses to him.

He sniffed a couple of times. "Interesting perfume you're wearing."

"Eau de perm solution. Grace nabbed me away from a curl job at the salon. Otherwise, I never would have come."

"Uh-huh."

She couldn't help noting that Nick, on the other hand, smelled of spicy male invitation. His jet-black hair had grown even longer. It pleased her that he hadn't had anyone else cut it. Which, she reminded herself, was dangerous, adolescent thinking. Turning her eyes toward the interview, she tried to ignore him.

Bunny was asking a sprightly question. "Ms. Hudson, why don't you tell me the history behind your costume."

With equal sprightliness, Grace complied. "It was my grandmother's travelin' dress, from around the turn of the century. My grandfather had built the ranch into a cattle spread, and Grandma was quite a clotheshorse, so . . ."

Carla had heard the story before, so she studied the interviewer's aerobically perfect body, expertly made-up face, and waterfall of blonde hair. She doubted the vibrant colors of her jumpsuit and chunky jewelry would ever hit the local shops. "So that's the infamous Bunny," she whispered, glancing at Nick.

He grinned. "Your basic girl next door."

She quirked up one corner of her mouth. "Looks pretty La La Land to me."

"Is a little old green-eyed demon shining through?"

"Why should I be jealous? I chose to leave that kind of life behind." She recrossed her legs, wishing she had anything on but a sexless divided skirt.

Grace rambled on about the past. "Old Chief Charlo and his people used to set up their tepees on my grandfather's land and dig the bitterroots they used for a staple food."

"Hear that?" Carla whispered. "He couldn't have been quite the bigot you'd like me to believe."

"The story line may not have run directly from point *A*, but it still reached point *B*." Nick lowered his stool to all four legs, placing his hands on his thighs. "I take it you haven't revealed the plot to Grace, seeing as she's not only here but looking friendly."

She lifted her shoulders. "I'm a coward, I guess."

"I offered to back you up, but I haven't been able to catch you to follow through. You're harder to track down than a CIA agent. Perchance, have you been avoiding me?"

She glanced at his knowing black eyes and breathed a laugh through her nose. "Darn right I have. Now be quiet, I'm trying to listen to Grace's interview."

"White people called that tribe of Indians the Flatheads. But they called themselves Salish, and thought of the Bitterroot Valley as their ancestral home." Grace added in a stage whisper, "Chief Charlo and his tribe were shafted by the government, you know."

Nick glanced at Carla. "Hear that? I'll bet she'll sympathize with my project, when *we* get around to telling her. That's one for the Indians." He jabbed his chest with a thumb.

"I wouldn't start counting yet, *kemo sabe*."

He laughed softly. "We shall see what we shall see."

After watching the old woman for a moment, he turned and studied Carla's face. "I'll bet Amazing Grace looked just like you when she was young.

Must be interesting to know what you'll look like when you get old."

She glanced at her aunt. They shared the Hudson high cheekbones, widely spaced eyes, and pointed chin, only Grace's face was weathered and wrinkled. "Oh, thanks, that's just what I needed—a foreshadowing of my aging, on top of everything else."

"I'm pointing out that she's a handsome woman." His gaze imprinted each of Carla's features with heat. "Which means you'll still be beautiful in sixty years too."

A reluctant smile blossomed on her face. "You do have a smooth, innovative line, I'll give you that," she whispered. "But don't lay it on too thick—make it fifty years from now, not sixty; I'm no kid."

"I'm partial to mature women." Nick grinned, then cocked a brow at Carla. "Aren't you auditioning too?"

"Good Lord, no! Don't try to tell me these auditions aren't a PR ploy to butter up the community. Casting will choose a few token extras, and probably have a great old time laughing at the 'local yokels' on the rest of the video."

"Ouch." Nick winced. "Why in the devil are you so convinced the movie industry is out to snooker you? What'll it take to make you trust me?"

Just then Bunny shaded her eyes from the spotlights and looked into their corner. "Nicky, are you still there?" she called out. "Are you aware of the potential of Ms. Hudson's historical props and information?"

Carla stared at the beautiful woman, then rose to her feet, spurred by an irrational sense of hurt. "Um-*hmmm*, let's all trust *Nicky*, shall we?"

"Damn!" He grabbed her arm. "Wait, give me a chance to explain."

"No need to explain anything to me, *Nicholas*," she said icily. "It's none of my business what you do with whom. My concern is that *I* don't fall for your little Nicky games."

Twisting free, Carla walked away from him with stiff-spined dignity and followed Grace to the door.

Nick was still sitting on the stool, propped against the wall, when things wound down. None of the other auditions had penetrated his consciousness after Carla had lopped him off. He was so preoccupied, he didn't notice everyone leave and the spotlights go off, didn't even hear Bunny snapping her gum as she gathered up the results.

He'd scrupulously avoided sticky relationships with women after . . . For the last ten years he'd flitted from one flatteringly eager beauty to another, the eternal butterfly. But he didn't have a shred of resistance to Carla. While she seemed determined to teach him what losing felt like.

It was almost six when Preston Mann popped his head in and called out, "I see you guys finished taping the local—"

Nick cut him off by bringing his stool down on its legs with a crash. "Pres, if you say local yokels one time, I'll sue for breach of contract and withdraw my screenplay."

Preston jerked a thumb and asked, "What's with Nicky?"

"Your guess is as good as mine," Bunny said, sorting through her precise shorthand notes. "A woman came in and sat with him for a while, and he's been pouting ever since she left."

Pres walked into the center of the room. "Could it be his love life has gone sour? Can the invincible fall?"

"Not funny, Pres," Nick said petulantly, confident his friends would forgive his snit; they'd supported each other through various crises for ten years. "I just wish I knew what in the devil I'm doing wrong."

"Let's get at the facts—what's she like?"

A sunburst went off in Nick's chest when he

pictured Carla. "Tender . . . full of life, perky, funny. She's got big eyes of the most unusual violet color. She's got this fantastic neck and . . ." He could still feel it under his lips. A dreamy smile lit his face.

"Sounds like a nice, likable person," Bunny commented from the depths of her paper-shuffling. "So naturally you tried to talk her into going to bed with you first thing, being a typical testosterone-fueled male."

"I did not." He thought for a moment, then winced. "Maybe I teased her a little, but I didn't push anything."

"Mmm-*hmmm!* Then how is it you've been reduced to pouting in corners, Nicky, darling?"

"For Pete's sake, don't call me Nicky!"

"Why not? It's your name, isn't it?"

"Well . . . it's hard to explain," he muttered, cursing himself for getting into such a frustrating tangle.

At the sound of his deep sigh, she squinted at him. "Are you serious about this woman?"

Nick jumped up to pace around the room. "I don't know! It's like I'm suffering from an *obsession.* I've never felt this way before, and I never wanted to. I can't figure out why or how. It's like something psychic is pulling us together. Destiny, or karma . . . past lives . . . whatever."

Pres lifted his brows toward Bunny. "What language is this man speaking?"

"He lost me back at 'obsession.'" She blew a bubble, shaking her head, and popped it in her mouth. "Really, Nick. *Psychic destiny?*"

He shrugged sheepishly over having said something so impassioned. "Well, I've never run into anything like this."

Pres studied him. "Sounds like love to me."

Bunny sniffed. "Not everyone has to be in love. Just because you get married again and again and again, and again, Preston, you think it's universal. You're an incurable romantic."

"Better an incurable romantic than a living computer with a floppy disk for a brain. I hope I'm around to rub it in when the bug finally bites you. If the invincible Nick can fall, so can you."

Nick scowled over the good-natured squabbling. "I have not fallen in love!" He didn't like to admit even to his best friends that the idea scared the starch out of him. "There isn't any room in my life for love."

Pres watched him pace restlessly. "You've been gadding around the world ever since I met you, Nicky. Is it possible you've finally found what you've been searching for?"

"I haven't been searching for anything!" Nick paused a moment, wondering if . . . maybe . . . then shook his head. "Anyway, even if I had found the winning ticket, this lady won't have anything to do with me at all, no way, no how."

Bunny tossed back her mane of blonde hair and smiled. "Which makes her unique, and therefore incredibly desirable. Who *is* she?"

He threw himself down on a chair beside the table and supported his head on his hands. "Grace Hudson's niece."

"Oh, sure, I know her well," Pres said. "I dated her sister for a while between marriages. Pretty, naive little thing, thought she wanted to be an actress. I meant to ask Carla whatever happened to Janet, but I haven't seen her since we arrived."

"She's skulking around to avoid me." Nick lifted his chin. "Seems as if I remember her saying her sister died."

Preston's face fell. "Oh, no! *How?*"

"She didn't say."

"Why's this Carla so down on you?" Bunny asked.

Nick scrubbed his hands over his face. "She doesn't like my lifestyle, and hates my project, as well as having a major grudge against the movie industry in general."

"Why don't you give up the lost cause, Nicky?"

Pres suggested. "There are several groupies circling around the company, dying for attention."

"Wait a minute." Bunny held up a hand. "Let's examine the data first. What are you expecting from your obsession? A roll in the sheets? A permanent relationship? If so, would she gad about with you in your travels? Or would a sophisticated man like you try to make a life in this rural valley?"

Sweat popped out on his forehead. "Jeez, Bunny, aren't you being a little premature? The woman won't even go out to dinner with me."

She studied him sympathetically. "Have you considered openly, honestly telling her what makes Nicky run? Maybe if she understood why—"

"*No!*" An icicle stabbed at his heart.

"Then I vote with Pres—go find a bimbo instead."

Scowling, Nick thought about letting Carla know him for what he really was. Lay himself out on a butcher's block for dissection. He'd faced all kinds of danger; a grizzly bear couldn't faze him. But it would take a different kind of courage to face scorn—or worse, pity—in Carla's eyes.

Of course, he didn't like the alternative either: backing out and letting her go. His heart seemed to turn itself inside out as he pictured her in his mind—her laugh, her quick wit, her lush body. *Her neck.*

"Dammit!" he said with a growl, jumping up to stride toward the door. "I refuse to give up!"

Carla had sunk into a venomous mood by the time she flipped the sign in the door, closing Hudson's Hair. Ever since leaving the auditions she'd fought a mental image of Nick—*Nicky!*—with the glamorous Bunny. "*What difference does it make!*" she exclaimed, pressing her forehead against the cool glass of the window.

Gazing out at the deserted street of the small town,

she conceded that she might have been somewhat bored with life in the valley before Nick came along. But she'd been content, and now her life was in such a turmoil, she didn't know what she wanted any longer.

Blinded by introspection, she jumped, startled when something—a giant moth?—batted at her face from the other side of the glass. Not a moth, a white rose. In the hand of . . . "Go away, Nick!" she called through the window.

He circled the flower on the glass in front of her face. "We need to talk."

She steeled herself against desire and longing. "We don't have anything to say to each other."

"Yes we do." His features set themselves stubbornly as he turned to stride toward the door.

Carla ran across the room, but he easily pushed the door open against her weight before she could turn the lock. "What do you think you're *doing*?" she cried.

He advanced mulishly with the white rose held in his fist. "I'm going to, by gosh, hand over this flag of truce, whether you want it or not."

Retreating, she clasped her hands just as mulishly behind her back. "Surely you have more productive things to do than terrorize me!"

"No, as a matter of fact, I don't."

When she wouldn't accept the flower, Nick put it in a coffee cup and set it on the counter at her station, the long stem leaning perilously to the side. Then he climbed into the styling chair and planted himself for a stay, hooking his boot heels on the footrest, tweaking up the legs of his jeans, and arching his muscular body to tuck down his shirt. "I need a haircut. You said it yourself—I look shaggy."

Carla stood beside the door, arms folded across her midriff, flushed with the rebelliously excited racing of her heart. "I'm closed for the night. I just cleaned the place up and I'm tired."

Putting a foot on the floor, Nick swiveled the chair around to face her. "Then we'll go have dinner together instead. But we *are* going to talk."

Apparently he was determined, so Carla calculated that dinner might take an hour, and a haircut only twenty minutes; she was more likely to be able to resist him for the latter. "Oh, all right," she said, walking forward to whip a cape over the more disturbing areas of his body.

His crisp hair clung when she ran her fingers into it, the seductive sensation twining through her body. Literally itching to get the job done as quickly as possible, she water-spritzed his hair, sectioned it, and began snipping the side. "Well, *Nicky*," she said snidely, "what was it we needed to talk about so urgently?" The green-eyed demon induced her to add, "Bunny?"

He winced as the dart hit. "Yes, Bunny. It didn't mean anything when she called me Nicky. She's just a friend, and all my friends call me Nicky."

"Oh, give me a break—I wasn't born yesterday. Men aren't *friends* with women who look like Bunny!" she snapped, her scissors flying. "If all your friends call you Nicky, then why did you make it sound like a proposition in my case?"

"It wasn't a proposition!"

Shoving his head forward, she spritzed the back of his head with enough force to mist the plants hanging six feet beyond. "How am I supposed to believe that? You've been telling me exactly what suits your fancy all along."

"Okay, maybe it was a proposition, sort of," he admitted. "Mostly I was running off at the mouth because you're so quick on the uptake. What can I say? The devil made me do it, I guess."

"I don't care if it was King Farouk who made you do it. I don't appreciate being seen as another gullible tootsie, along with your many others," she said, layering his hair in back. "So why don't you concentrate on Bunny and leave me alone."

"Open and honest," Nick whispered to himself, then took a deep breath. "Look, okay, maybe there was a little something between Bunny and me once, but it was twelve years ago, way back in college when we first met."

The idea was offensive enough to lend power to Carla's fingers as she began snipping his other side. "I have no interest in hearing the sordid details of your affairs!"

"I didn't *intend* to tell you them!" Nick bent an eye at the furiously clacking scissors, as if wishing he could suck in his vulnerable ear. "All I intended to tell you is that we were as incompatible as hell. Bunny functions on the genius level, and I'm—" He caught his upper lip with his lower teeth, then said, "Well, with my learning disabilities I'm not an Einstein. She read for me in college. We didn't click, but we liked each other and stayed friends. That's all there is to it."

Scissors motionless, brows elevated under her tousled chestnut bangs, Carla stared at his reflection and repeated the two words he had dropped so casually. "Learning disabilities? *You?*"

"Woof! Being open and honest isn't as easy as it sounds." Nick batted at the underside of the cape as if he felt imprisoned, then freed a hand to touch the scar on his brow. "When you asked how I got this, I didn't tell the whole story."

Carla studied his face, her anger evaporating; she could see something was bothering him terribly. "It isn't necessary for me to know all your secrets, Nick."

"Yes, it is. I should start by saying my parents are both successful professional people, so they assumed their progeny would be a motivated overachiever like themselves." He gave a short laugh. "I threw twenty different kinds of monkey wrenches into their lives when I came along—a raving, hyper-active dyslexic. Oh, they loved me—still do, for that matter. But they didn't have either the time or inclination to cope with me, so they sent me to boarding schools specializing in learning-disabled children."

The fierce look on his face defied sympathy, so she said simply, "You're obviously an intelligent, edu-cated, successful man, so you must have overcome your difficulties."

"Maybe I did, and maybe I didn't." A tornado of hair clippings flew off the cape when Nick heaved up in the chair, crossing his knees. "I still can't read worth a damn," he admitted, grimacing. "The letters crawl around on the paper. Maybe if someone high-lights the finer points with a yellow marker pen, I can catch the drift."

Caught by surprise, Carla stared at him. "You can't read?"

His eyes narrowed. "Are we going to feel sorry for poor slow Nicky now?"

The tone of his voice stung, and Carla jerked her chin up. "*I'm* not! Do you feel sorry for yourself?"

"No, just embarrassed."

Carla's indignation had sent relief washing over his face, and she sensed he feared pity. "Why should you feel embarrassed? Good grief, I *can* read, and I haven't done a tenth as well with my life as you have with yours. How'd you manage?"

"I gave up the rebellion and began learning after I ran into a teacher who showed me I had talents I could develop. I got through college by hiring people to read my books and papers to me. Bunny was one, and now she's my interpreter in the Enterprise. I wrote the screenplay by tape recorder, that sort of thing." He shrugged slightly. "I've learned how to pass. But I still feel more at home with the ramblin' life than butting heads in the intellectual world."

Now Carla understood the loneliness she sensed in

him occasionally. "Such as running after Amazon Indians and wandering around the wilderness doing films?"

He nodded, tunneling his hand back under the cape. "Childhood was pretty lonely and frustrating, so I lived for my summers of bumming around with my granddad. I went into photography because it was a way to support the life of wanderlust he taught me to love."

"Is he still alive?" Carla asked, blessing the man for having understood and accepted the young Nick.

He gave an affectionate laugh. "Alive and kicking at eighty-five, and grouching because he couldn't make the last segment of old Pierre's trail with me. I gave him a video of the Salmon River trek when I went back to LA."

She smiled. "You must love him as much as I love Grace."

"Then you must love her a lot." He gazed into Carla's face with his dark, soul-searching eyes. "I wrote the screenplay for him, because he was always there for me. That's why the movie is so important to me."

Tears started up in her eyes. "You're a lovely, sweet person to do something so beautiful for an old man."

"Let's not make a saint out of me." Nick pulled his mouth up in a self-conscious grimace. "I just wanted you to know there's a reason for who I am and what I'm doing, even though you hate the movie so."

She nodded slightly, then touched his shoulder. "I'm glad you told me about yourself, Nick. I feel as if you're so much more . . . I don't know . . . real. You can be pretty overwhelming, you know."

Cockiness crept back into his grin. "It's my intention to keep you overwhelmed and . . . uh . . . pliable."

Laughing, she snapped her scissor blades. "Sorry

to disillusion you, but I'm . . . uh . . . hard as nails."

"We shall see about that." His eyes gleamed midnight dark. "Anyhow, I hope this long-drawn-out true confession of mine has convinced you there's nothing romantic going on between Bunny and me."

"Okay, she's just a buddy," Carla conceded. "But I can't imagine why it's so important that I believe you."

"Because I don't want you to think all I wanted was to jump in the sack with you. For me to be this interested in someone, there's got to be more to it than that."

Her brows came down over the new concept, and she stepped forward and began snipping at his hair again, far more gently now. "You made an issue of not being permanent when we first met—are you changing your story?"

"Well-l-l . . ."

"Well-l-l, indeed."

"Okay, you've made your point!" He hitched himself up in the chair and turned his head to look directly at her. "Does my little problem with reading turn you off?"

Surprised by the question, she grinned. "I have laid awake more than one or two nights thinking about you since we met." She glanced pointedly at his broad shoulders and the rest of the body under the cape. "But it wasn't because I wondered whether you could read or not."

"Thank you," Nick said quietly. "I needed to hear you say that, because I've never met a woman who intrigued me as much as you do, Carla." The heat of his midnight eyes lit fires as his gaze moved slowly around her face, touching her violet eyes, her upturned nose, the fullness of her lips. "Ever since the first night, I've been fascinated to distraction."

She looked down to escape the tender trap of his gaze, not certain how she wanted to respond to his new seriousness. It had been simple to flare up and resist his sassy flirting. But now they seemed poised on the brink of a new phase.

When she didn't answer, he said, "You're obsessed with me, too, aren't you? I can see it in your face."

She nodded, thumbing the teeth of the comb. "You're on my mind all the time. . . . I care a lot more about you than I want to, or than is good for me." She glanced up, smiling with tremulous lips. "I've never felt like this about anyone else. But I don't know where it's going, and I'm scared."

He studied her, frowning. "I know; it's new territory for me too."

Shivery with apprehension—or was it anticipation?—Carla picked the white rose out of the cup and touched it to her nose. Her feelings were skyrocketing and she needed time to bring them down to reality. Walking to the back room, she filled a bud vase with water, thinking about the little boy Nick had been. Her heart was full, knowing him at last, and liking him so much better for it. On the other hand, the implications of his background were deeply troubling. She'd thought before that he traveled for fun. Now she saw that it was necessary to escape a world in which he didn't feel comfortable. Not choice at all.

Carla put the rose in the vase and walked slowly back to her station. "Thanks for bringing such a sweet flag of truce," she said almost shyly. "I'm embarrassed to have acted like a juvenile idiot over Bunny."

His face came to life with an engaging smile. "Your jealousy told me you care. I needed to know that."

Taking up her scissors, she began shaping the top of his head. Her body was inches away from his, brushing his elbow, setting off flares of desire. "We're a homebody and a rover, absolutely impossible for each other," she said breathlessly. "It doesn't make sense for this to happen. It seems almost as if something is pushing us together."

Nick had his eyes pinched shut against the falling hair. "Mmm-hmmm. Remember, I told you fate had its eye on us. Better than that, there's magic between us."

"Magic?" Lips parted, she stilled her scissors and looked down at the thick black lashes that fanned over his cheeks. "More likely some good, lusty chemistry," she said. "Or the novelty of meeting someone new."

"You aren't just new, you're unique." Nick squinted his eyes open, cautious of the snippings. "We could put it to the test. Chemistry and novelty don't last, but magic survives everything. I've got lots of time for a thorough testing of . . . uh . . . things. How about you?"

A bud of excitement began growing in Carla's body, then unfolding into a full bloom of desires, needs, and demands. Running her fingertips over his face, she brushed hair off his lean cheeks, out of the dimple in his chin, letting her touch linger over his mouth. A smile curved her lips. "Could those . . . uh . . . 'things' be related to . . . uh . . . whoopee?"

He grinned under her fingertips. "Some of that, I expect, but we also need to spend a lot of time finding out what makes each other tick."

Nodding slowly, she ran a finger down his nose, then withdrew and pressed her hand flat against her chest. It frightened her to think of going into an affair that would surely have no happy ending. "I'm tied down and my time is tight. That's how I tick."

"Surely you have a spare moment here or there." He read her face and smiled. "I can see in your eyes that you're as excited as I am about . . . uh . . . in-depth research."

"Don't we all want things that aren't good for us?" Carla said, laughing softly.

He laughed, too, lifting his brows. "We won't know what's good until we examine the situation."

"Mmm-m-m," she commented, leaning against the arm of the chair to snip tag ends from his hair.

After a few moments she became aware of the sensuality simmering below the surface of his face and in the tension of his body; he was aroused by her nearness. He could easily have seduced her into a decision. The fact that he hadn't convinced her to step through the door he'd been so patiently holding open. "Yes, I think we should find out what's going on with us."

His smile was a sunburst. Freeing a hand from the cape, he ran his fingertips down the curve of her neck and circled his hand around her nape, urging her mouth down toward his parted, inviting lips. He claimed her as his own, probing her mouth, his tongue jousting with hers. The sweetness of his scent entered her every pore. His fresh, excited breath mingled with hers.

Carla drew away because she thought her body might burst into flames. Every synapse in her brain was firing off-kilter. "Hi," she whispered inanely.

"Hi," Nick answered with a tremulous smile. "That was some start. When might you have another few minutes of time to go on with this research?"

"I might have tomorrow off."

"What would you like to do?"

Do? There were a hundred interesting suggestions in his eyes, and she was tempted. "I need to go slow and easy before making the leap, that's what I'd like to do."

He nodded. "Okay, one day at a time."

She smiled like an idiot at him, and he smiled like a moron right back. "Let's do something outside, as long as you don't expect me to visit Little Hollywood," she said. "I'm not interested in rejoining life on the fast track."

"Okay, how about if we nose around the back end

of the ranch on horseback and you help me look for old Pierre's cabin?"

"Sure." Carla brushed him off and removed the cape, then brought out the broom to sweep up a mound of black hair. She glanced up teasingly. "In fact, I think it's a wonderful idea to cover every inch of the ranch, just to prove Pierre never lived on the Hudson holdings. Then I won't have to explain your screenplay to Grace."

"I offered to help you tell her," he reminded her again, climbing out of the chair to hold the dustpan.

"All right, I accept, camera bum. It's only fair you should play black-hat bad guy, while I play white-hat faithful niece, ready to pick up the pieces when she blows."

Nick laughed, and they walked to the door. "How much do I owe you for the haircut?" he asked.

"You paid enough for the first haircut to last the lifetime of your lease."

Stepping forward, he cupped her head between his two hands, running his fingers up into her short, tousled hair. "I'm more interested in a lease on you."

Slowly, he feathered his lips around her face until his mouth settled over hers. She could feel his sensuality simmering and stewing for release. Matching heat exploded through her body. Drawing away, she took a deep, quavery breath. "One day at a time . . . remember?"

Trailing kisses down her neck and around the base of her throat, he whispered, "And every day a jewel in a necklace of weeks, months."

She shivered over the sensation of his lips on her skin. "I must be in trouble if you're turning poetic, Ni—*Nick*."

He gave his chuckling, irrepressible laugh. "Things are looking up—you almost called me Nicky."

"This is ridiculous!" she exclaimed, pulling away. "I'm going home."

He trailed his fingers down her arms. "I'll come along and help out with Grace. Or . . . whatever."

"No," she said, her heart swelling to the danger point of desire. "I need time to think. I'm not ready for either Grace or 'whatever' tonight. Morning is soon enough. Come over to the ranch house at ten or so."

After locking up the shop, Carla fled into the dusk, trying to escape the tantalizing sensation of Nick's kisses lingering on her neck. Fumbling with her keys, she knew she couldn't resist the magic pulling them together much longer. But she was so confused.

Her heart ached for the troubled boy he had been; she admired and liked the man he'd become. But the child being the seed of the man, she understood and accepted the fact that he could never be a forever man.

Five

The next morning, Carla came downstairs to the kitchen all dressed and ready for riding long before nine o'clock. Grace was sitting at the table in baggy pants and a brightly patterned blouse, doing the crossword puzzle in the daily newspaper. "Mornin', dear," she greeted without glancing up. "Thought you had today off."

"I do."

"Well, ain't you turnin' into a regular early bird."

"Couldn't sleep—I tossed and turned all night." Carla poured a cup of coffee and stood by the pot, enjoying the first enlivening swallows.

"Lester's an even earlier riser, so breakfast came and went a long time ago. He might be a lot of questionable things, but he never was lazy." Grace gazed out the window, watching the old handyman, mounted on a tractor-mower, *putt-putt-putting* around the acre of patchy lawn surrounding the house. "Papa never could stand a slugabed."

"Good old Papa," Carla muttered, wondering how Grace would respond to hearing that the movie would be a family exposé. She opened the refrigerator to ponder an array of country food. "By the way, Nick Leclerc is dropping in later this morning."

Her aunt jotted a word into the puzzle. "I thought you were avoidin' him."

"Well . . . not any longer, I guess."

"Something romantic goin' on in that neck of the woods?"

"I'm not sure; there might be." Carla braced her arm on top of the fridge door, her stomach churning at the sight of various neatly stowed leftovers. "We seem to be awfully attracted, but we aren't very well suited to each other."

"Never known that to stop anyone from wantin'." Grace gazed out the window, tapping her pencil in time with the putting of Lester's mower. "You're lucky things are a little looser nowadays. Take it from me, there ain't any less pain in thinkin' back on might-have-beens after abstainin'. Might as well partake."

Carla glanced at her aunt, surprised that so liberal a comment should come from a distance of two generations. "What *did* happen between you and Lester when you were young?"

"That doesn't have a thing to do with this!" Grace gave an exasperated grunt and threw down her pencil, which rolled off the table and clattered across the floor. "Now will you get yourself outta the icebox before you burn out the motor! I'll fix you some eggs and toast."

Carla closed the refrigerator without taking anything out and refilled her cup with coffee. "Thanks, Auntie, but I couldn't eat—my stomach is tied in knots."

"If you don't start eatin' decent, you're gonna—"

Grace broke off when she got her first good look at Carla, taking in her delicate pink shirt and knee-high riding boots. Her white brows shot up as she stared skeptically at the cream stretch breeches hugging Carla's curvaceous body like another skin. "Judas Priest! What kind of outfit is that?!"

"English riding clothes—I should by all rights wear

a jacket and hat, too, but it's too hot for them. I used to wear this outfit when I took jumping and dressage lessons back in California, and I wanted to look a teeny bit more sophisticated than I usually do, because all Nick has ever seen me in are my working clothes." Carla looked down at herself ambivalently. "Do you think I look funny?"

"You're more apt to singe the man's ears off than make him laugh."

Before she could decide whether to change or not, Pip's barking heralded the arrival of company, the noise advancing onto the back stoop, punctuated by a knock.

Her heart thumping an excited tango, she opened the screen. Pip bulled his way past her legs before she could react. "You dumb dog, get back outdoors," she cried, grabbing and missing as he scrabbled across the linoleum. Embedding himself under the table, he planted his muzzle defiantly on his front paws.

Outside the door, Nick gave a whoop of laughter. "I watched the bloodthirsty beast plan that maneuver before you came to the door. He knows exactly how to get around you."

"I have a feeling he's not the only one who does," Carla said with a flustered grin. "But come in anyway."

Stepping into the kitchen with an accordion-pleated folder in his hand, Nick ran a randy-eyed look down her outfit, lingering over the elastic breeches. "Hey, I thought I was going out for a ride with a little old country girl this morning. Who's this lady royale? Wow!"

Carla laughed, half-embarrassed, half-pleased over the effect she'd caused, and said, "Wow, yourself," after looking him up and down in return. His western shirt and pants were almost as form-fitting as her outfit, and he had brand-new embossed cowboy boots on his feet. "Good try, but you're never going to look much like a little old country boy, camera bum."

He gave a sassy wink, then turned to Grace. "Since we're passing compliments around, you're looking lovely, too, Ms. Hudson."

"Women of my age look well-preserved at best, and I ain't no Miz. I'm *Miss* Hudson, not ashamed of it, and too damn smart to be waltzed around," she said, frostily mistrustful of his velvety voice and beguiling smile. "Got your ears lowered, I see."

He combed fingers through his shorn hair. "Yes, ma'am, Miss Hudson." Dark eyes twinkling, he tacked on a murmur: "Amazing Grace."

"Humph!" she grunted, a matching gleam in her faded blue eyes. "Carla refused my offer of breakfast; want me to throw you a bone?"

Nick rubbed his lean belly. "Thanks, but I couldn't eat a thing—for some reason my stomach feels all tied up this morning."

"Seems to me there must be some kind of flu goin' around," Grace said slyly, picking up her puzzle and eyeing the pencil on the floor. "I better take myself elsewhere so I don't catch it."

"You two are perfect equals when it comes to waltzing people around," Carla said, laughing. "Stay sat, Auntie, Nick came to see you, not me. He's going to tell you all about the—"

"Actually," he broke in, taking several tattered daguerreotypes out of his folder, "I'm going to show you some pictures of my family. They used to live in the Bitterroot Valley a long time ago. This is my great-great-grandfather, Pierre Leclerc."

Grace peered at the picture through her bifocals. "Looks like a real desperado in that beard, don't he?"

Carla leaned over her shoulder and gave a hoot of laughter. "He looks exactly like Nick did, the first time I saw him."

"I'm surprised you didn't run screaming," he said.

"I have a feeling I should have."

Grace beetled her brows. "I don't recognize him."

"You wouldn't; he was a trapper from long before your time," he said. "But he did settle in the valley for a while and scratched out the beginnings of a ranch. He sent his oldest son, Michel, back to France, where he became an artist of sorts." Nick took a miniature in an oval frame out of the folder. "Michel did this watercolor of a woman he loved, apparently from memory years and years after they'd parted. I guess he never forgot her."

Grace took the painting in arthritis-warped fingers and stared at it with surprise. "Why, land's sake this is a pitcher of my Aunt Emily!"

"*What?!*" Carla peered over Grace's shoulder. The painting was of a young woman, hardly more than a girl, with fair hair drawn back by a bow, her kitten face unmistakably Hudson. "Where did this Aunt Emily come from, Auntie? You've never mentioned her."

Grace snorted a laugh. "No one dared talk about her after she struck up too cozy a friendship with a half-breed boy, incurrin' the wrath of her father, my grandfather. He was a mean old bastard—got rid of the boy and sent Emily back to live with Ohio relatives. I met her several times when I visited. Sweet, gentle woman . . . never got married, though she was some looker." She set the painting on the table, squared it up, and glanced at Nick. "The half-breed boy was Michel, was he?"

He nodded cautiously, then plunged in: "The movie we're filming is the story of Emily and Michel. Names changed, of course."

Grace scowled at him for what seemed minutes, rolling that around in her mind. Finally she said, "Well, they better be doin' it with respect."

"I'm here to see that they do."

Carla's chin dropped; then she sat down. "Auntie, you mean there's something *to* the story that your grandfather took this ranch away from old Pierre Leclerc?!"

"Well, shoot!" Grace said, looking puzzled. "That's no secret. It's nothin' to be proud of, but everyone around here knows the first Hudson ran rampant over some toes."

"No one ever told *me*!"

The old woman reached out and patted Carla's hand. "I didn't think you could handle hearing. You have such a glorified view of our family."

"*I* have a glorified view of—" Carla bent her head forward and peered at her aunt. "Don't you *mind* them making a movie about your family's shady past?"

"Mind!" Something close to a simper puckered Grace's wrinkled face. "The movie's gonna put the Bitterroot Valley on the map. If it's really about the Hudsons, why, I'll be the envy of the community."

After staring at her aunt for a few seconds, Carla rose to her feet, took a handful of carrots out of the fridge, and walked toward the door, glancing at Nick with narrowed eyes. "I, for one, am going for that ride now. Only if certain persons can resist gloating are they welcome to come with me."

He got up and followed, his face red with the glee he was controlling only by enormous effort. It took a moment before he could manage to say, "Certain persons are so delighted at the prospect, they won't say a word."

Carla walked with chin-lifted dignity to the door. Pip had been lying so quietly under the table, she'd forgotten he was there. When she opened the screen, he streaked past her legs in a bid to be first out the door. "Darn you, Pip!" she cried, dancing for balance.

Nick caught her with one arm around her shoulders, another around her waist, and looked down into her face with devilishly gleaming eyes. "This is the damnedest household."

"Before you came along it was perfectly normal and . . ." She'd turned so soft and breathless at his touch that she couldn't finish.

"Boring?" he said.

It was so true, she laughed softly. "Honestly, Nick—"

"Nicky." The laughter dancing in his eyes made the implicit invitation almost irresistible.

"Honestly, *Nicholas*, your ego and impudence never cease to amaze me!" Her arms itched to curl around the broad shoulders spreading out in front of her eyes. She restrained herself only because when she glanced sidelong at Grace, her aunt was peering sidelong back with a sagacious grin on her walnut face.

"We're going riding, Auntie," she announced, stressing the "riding," and freed herself from Nick's embrace.

"Su-u-u-re you are. You all have fun, hear? But don't do anything I wouldn't do."

"One of these days I'm going to pin you down and find out how much you would or wouldn't, or have or haven't done."

"Get your sassy mouth out of here!" Grace said, pursing her lips and picking up Nick's old pictures again.

Carla laughed and ran down the steps. The day was glorious, sunny, with a hint of ripe autumn in the air. The Big Sky of Montana stretched forever, as blue as it ever got. Mountains jutted up all around, giving the valley a sense of intimate privacy.

But Carla was aware only of the vigorous, masculine presence of Nick right behind her. Her feet seemed to float on air and her heart beat in double time as they walked side by side toward the barn. She had no idea what would happen during the day, but every instinct cried out that it would be more than a ride. And she felt lighter and more joyful than she could ever remember feeling. The whispers of excitement curling through the air were so urgent, they almost seemed real.

A big, rangy buckskin with a black mane and tail was drowsing in the corral, fitted out with saddle-bags and a rolled blanket as well as the usual tack. "This is my buddy," Nick said. "Who—perhaps not eagerly, but faithfully—carried me all the way along the Salmon River."

"Oh, isn't he a beauty." Carla opened the gate and walked toward the gelding, holding out a carrot. After eating it, the enormous horse nibbled her cheek with a velvety lip. When Pip stood on his hind legs, curious about the stranger, he touched noses with the horse and snorted. Carla smiled and glanced back at Nick. "I think these two are going to be friends."

He had both feet on the bottom rail of the corral, elbows crossed on the top, gazing meltingly at her. "They probably recognize each other as kindred spirits. Bloodthirsty beasts, both of them."

"How you talk! This big fellow acts mellow enough. What's his name?"

"Spook, for the record. Depending on the mood of the rider, he's more commonly called anything from bastard to SOB, and several less complimentary names too nasty to mention."

She laughed, familiar enough with horses to know that looks could be deceiving. "This bodes for an interesting ride, so let's get the show on the road."

Stepping out of the corral, Carla put two fingers in her mouth and let out a shrill whistle, bringing a black mare galloping in from the pasture, greedy for an accustomed carrot. "This is Molly, with nary an SOB bone in her body."

She put an English saddle on Molly, instead of her usual western one, and after mounting, rode a few yards down the lane before turning the mare to watch curiously as Nick led Spook out of the corral. She gasped when he swung into the saddle and the mellow buckskin exploded into a bucking, wheeling tornado.

"Settle down!" Nick bellowed, wrapping his long legs around the belly of the horse, clearly up to the challenge.

The flurry transformed Pip into a whirling dervish, yelping at the top of his voice. Despite that, only seconds later the buckskin shook himself. The expression on his equine face might have been a smug grin if he'd been human.

Carla burst out laughing. "What was that about?"

Nick ran an affectionate hand down the neurotic horse's neck. "Don't ask me, but the crazy bastard does that every time I climb on his back. Lord only knows why I put up with the joker. Like you said about Pip, he grew on me."

It touched her to realize he was kind and forgiving, unlike many other men who might have beaten the animal into submission. Filled with a rush of tender emotion, she couldn't keep her eyes off Nick as they rode toward the mountains. He sat his horse with easy grace, spine curving gracefully into the saddle.

The atmosphere seemed to vibrate with anticipation. Everything seemed twice as intense as usual. The air was perfumed with the scent of ripening wheat fields. Killdeers minced along the ground with an excited piping that sang in Carla's veins and spurred her into kicking the black into a gallop. "Race you to the big pine up on the ridge," she called over her shoulder.

"Hey, no fair, you didn't give me any warning," Nick shouted, thundering after her.

Laughing and flushed, they pulled to a stop at the top of the rise. "You ride pretty good for a girl," he teased. "I had to push just to come out a neck ahead. Luckily Spook may be an SOB, but he has long legs and lots of determination when challenged."

"That's what you are," Carla said with a smile.

"What, an SOB?"

"Probably that, too, but I was thinking of long-legged and determined." A laugh of pure joy bubbled out. Her spirit soared as she glanced at his legs. Their smoothly muscled thighs curved over the buckskin's withers, allowing full appreciation of the area in between.

He grinned his challenge. "Do you like what you see?"

"Mm-m-m, I'll never tell." Wheeling the black mare, she galloped northwest, following an urgent subliminal pull.

Nick loped beside her and grabbed a rein, pulling Molly around to trot eastward on the ridge. "Let's go this way—I want to show you something interesting."

A few minutes later, Carla pulled to an abrupt stop at the brink of the ridge, staring down into the valley with fascination. Ten large tepees were circled in a village by the creek, protected by aspens and pines.

Scattered throughout the encampment were black-haired people, going about the business of primitive living. Naked children laughed and called out in play. Mongrel dogs tussled and snapped at each other. Women in fringed, beaded, deerskin dresses were gathered around stew pots bubbling over open fires. Bows and arrows, even spears, were within arm's reach of the men lounging about in feathers, breechcloths, and leather leggings, bare-chested in the summer heat.

Conversations in the Salish tongue carried to the top of the ridge, sounding very exotic. A man began singing a high chant, sending shivers through Carla. "It's like a haunting, isn't it?" she whispered, glancing at Nick. "The past come alive."

He smiled, pleased with her reaction. "Just like old Pierre's life is happening all over again."

"I feel like enough of an interloper, but the movie crews positioned around the outside with their cameras are an insult to the privacy of the village."

"It does seem that way, doesn't it? But the only reason the village is there in the first place is to film the exterior scenes. All the interiors have already been done back in Los Angeles."

"It's hard to believe it's only a set. Whoever did it is brilliant. Those people look absolutely authentic."

"They are authentic," Nick said, and cocked a brow at her. "As you'd know, if you hadn't been so hostile to the movie and trying to avoid me. They're Salish people from the Flathead reservation."

Carla stared down at the village. "Fascinating!"

"Yes, it was quite an experience auditioning up at Pablo. I even found some descendants of old Pierre, making them my kin. Some of them are down there now—home again."

As he said that a triumphant breeze tumbled the pine boughs overhead, causing Spook to jerk at the reins. Nick quieted him, and went on. "It made me feel humbled and proud to feel connected to those people, like my existence in this country is a little more justified than most Americans'." He glanced at Carla with a teasing look in his black eyes. "And it left me feeling a lot more justified to claim squatter's rights on this ranch too."

"Your native connection is so watered down, it wouldn't stand up in a glass." She snorted a laugh and turned to watch the activity below. "What scene are they filming?"

"First I'll have to give you a time frame. This is happening after the settlers took over the valley, making it almost impossible for the Indians to live by hunting and gathering, as they'd done for centuries. They're practically destitute. Michel has just met Emily, and in this scene he's wandering among his mother's tribal group, torn between two cultures, an outsider in both. The actor playing Michel is the young man with a headband around shoulder-length hair, the only one in shirt and pants. Over there by the sunburst tepee."

Squinting against the distance, Carla picked him out, then glanced at Nick. "Is he someone I should recognize?"

"No, the cast are all unknowns, since money is tight. It's a gamble, but they're talented."

Carla nodded. "Sometimes fresh blood makes a more powerful product."

She watched with interest as movie personnel and a camera mounted on the back of a truck moved to a new position at the edge of the encampment. A shoot tended to be boring and slow-moving, she knew, but the novelty of seeing it happen again after so many years sent tremors of excitement racing through her veins. "Oh, that's Preston Mann over there, isn't it?" She smiled and peered at the ginger-haired man. "I liked Pres a lot back when he and my sister—" Breaking off, she bit her lip over a surge of sadness.

Nick studied her face curiously for a few moments. "Want to go down and say hello to Pres?" he asked when she didn't go on.

"No, I'd rather not."

"Why?"

"I just don't want to, that's all."

The two horses whisked their tails and jingled their bridles at flies, and Pip lay panting by Spook's front legs, tongue lolling as moments of silence dragged. Finally Nick said, "I don't really know the first thing about you, Carla. Like what makes you happy or sad, or what your childhood was like. So I can't help wondering, why *did* you leave Los Angeles and movie life?"

Carla gave a goose-bumpy shiver. "It's too beautiful a day to go muckraking. All I want is to rest and relax, be with you, and think happy."

"But I told you my deepest darkest secret, so it's only fair for me to hear yours."

Carla stared down at the Indian encampment. Sure, she knew Nick's secrets, but not what his lonely childhood had done to his capacity to love. For that matter, she didn't know what *her* unhappy life had done to her capacity to accept happiness. "Lord knows what might pop out if I open up—Frankenstein's monster maybe," she said, trying to wiggle out of answering with a joke.

But he didn't laugh. "You know, I get the feeling you're a lot more excited about this movie than you want to admit. You miss being a part of the business, don't you?"

Carla cocked one leg up over Molly's shoulder and pulled at the inner loop on her tall boot. "I liked my work well enough, but that was another era, and it doesn't make any difference why I ended it. The important thing is that I have no interest in going back."

He continued studying her, trying to read what she was thinking and feeling. "I'm not sure I believe you. I think you're bored with life in the valley, and you didn't want the movie filmed here because you're scared to death you'll be seduced back into the life you left."

"All right, okay! Maybe I do have some mixed feelings about it, but I'd never, ever be seduced back again." She glanced at him with flaring violet eyes. "I fought the movie because I'm furious over the past nosing out my own personal speck of the earth, out of the entire map of the United States, and coming here to make me feel dissatisfied and restless over my choice."

Nick nudged the buckskin closer and took Carla's hand. "Those must be the first open, honest words I've heard you speak since I met you."

His hand was warm and strong, comforting; she threaded her fingers between his. "I haven't been lying to you. It's just that half the time I can't understand my own feelings and motives, much less explain them to someone else."

"Believe me, I know what you mean." Nick lifted

their joined hands to his lips and kissed her knuckles. "It's hard to face problems before you're ready." His lips twitched with a wry smile. "Maybe that's why you transferred your qualms over onto your aunt, who obviously has no qualms at all about the movie and her history."

Pulling her hand free, Carla cocked an eye at him and forced a laugh, backing away from seriousness. "I wondered how long it'd take before you started gloating over my off-base reading of Grace."

He grinned puckishly. "I thought I'd been restraining myself remarkably well."

"Then why don't you continue the valiant effort?"

Wheeling Molly, Carla headed away from the village, drawn again by her unexplained urge to aim toward the mountains in the northwest. "If you're so fired up about looking for old Pierre's cabin, let's get crackin'."

"I'm more fired up about you." Urging the buckskin closer, his leg brushing Carla's, he said, "It occurs to me that you didn't mention whether you liked what you saw when you looked me over a while back. What's the verdict?"

"I've since forgotten what you look like."

"Well, sweetie, here I am." He spread his arms, riding out Spook's restless prancing.

Carla grinned, happy enough for a chance to look him over again. She had prepared herself to cope with his body, but the bit of black hair peeking seductively out of the open neck of his shirt pushed her over the brink. Her body responded with a shuddering force that curled her toes and flushed her face. Displaying remarkable restraint, she flipped her hand back and forth. "I'd rate you, at the very least—so-so."

Nick threw back his head in a free laugh and swung the buckskin around, pulling the horses nose to tail, the people face to face. "It's dangerous to tease a man after looking at him with such hungry eyes," he said, entrapping her with his own rapacious, midnight gaze.

Her system went wild with sensation when he slid his hand up the taut breeches on her thigh and curved his fingers around the explosive area between her widely spread legs. "There's nothing so-so about what I've got under my hand," he said in a husky whisper.

Gasping a harsh breath, Carla grabbed the pommel of his saddle and turned toward him, wanting more of his hand, all of him. She laughed softly and whispered, "Actually you're at least a hundred percent better than so-so, too, Nick. I just didn't want to inflate your ego too far."

His thumb moved tantalizingly along the taut material over her crotch. "Sweetheart, I don't know about my ego, but you've inflated . . . uh . . . something."

Her eyes were instantly drawn to his fly. Surges of desire lit the soft core of her body; it was only with powerful force of will that she said, "I think we've carried this little tease too far. Slow and easy, remember?"

Though she said it, she didn't move away, and Nick pressed his hand urgently on her tender parts. "You don't want slow and easy any more than I do. I can feel how much you want me. You're throbbing." He gazed at her with molten lava in his eyes, waiting for her yes. "It doesn't have to be a tumble in the dust; I've got all the niceties—even a blanket, right here behind my saddle."

She was on the brink of giving in when Pip leaped up and yelped after a chipmunk, startling the horses. Carla and Nick were torn apart as Molly began dancing in circles and Spook tried a few token bucks.

When everything had settled down again, Carla gave a shaky laugh. "There you go, camera bum, a message from a higher source, telling us to slow down and think things out."

"Whatever the source," Nick said, still fighting the buckskin, "you're right, our lovemaking is too important to go at slapdash. But you *are* going to have me sooner or later, sweetheart. And, oh, baby, when you do there's going to be fireworks and heaven and the Ringling Brothers Circus, all tied up in one package."

With crazy feelings toppling head over heels in her mind, she swung Molly around and aimed northwest. Why she hadn't let Nick make love to her when she'd wanted it so badly was a puzzle without a solution. It wasn't as if she were a coy virgin. It simply hadn't seemed the right time . . . the right place.

Suddenly she kicked the black mare into a gallop. "Oh, I just remembered something! Come on, I think I know where the remains of old Pierre's cabin might be."

Six

Carla rode northwest as if drawn by a magnet. Following, Nick had not the slightest expectation of finding old Pierre's cabin after the passage of a century, but he surely did enjoy the search as he watched her shapely behind massaging the flat English saddle. His own western saddle was a torment to the urgency he'd been enduring ever since he'd put his hand on the lure between her legs.

It was a mystery to him why he'd let her get away from him when he'd had her in the palm of his hand—literally. He could have easily talked her into going the full way—she'd wanted him as badly as he'd wanted her. Maybe his problem was that for the first time in his life he cared enough to want to *know* a woman as a person before knowing her in the biblical sense. Dangerous thinking for a ramblin' man whose boyhood had conditioned him to never expect too much.

Carla reined in when they reached the base of a ramplike hill running up toward the mouth of the canyon, a creek rushing merrily around its base. "I thought this was the place, but it's at least eighteen years since I've been here. Janet and I found an old tumbledown cabin and played we were Davy Crockett huntin' b'ars." She turned that beguiling elfin smile of hers on him. "I told you I was a tomboy."

The notion delighted him. "Tomboys fit my lifestyle better than most."

She looked him up and down with a glint in her violet eyes. "Unlike some others I could mention, camera bum, I quit playing Davy Crockett a long, long time ago."

He glanced at the female body under her classy outfit. "I had no doubts whatever about that."

"My point is, I don't think this is the right place." She peered up the hill at thick pines and aspens that were already showing a hint of yellow in late August. "The going looks pretty rough. Maybe we should turn around and go home."

An irritated breeze swished through the trees, and Nick had no desire to cut short a day with Carla either. "Come on, we can't give up that easily. I'll lead the way." He clapped his hands against Spook's sides, sending the horse bounding forward, saddle-bags flopping, making trail through the brush by brute force.

Carla and the mare followed. When they reached a meadow near the top of the hill, two deer threw up their heads and bounded gracefully away. "Oh, how cunning!" she whispered. "I don't remember it being so beautiful here."

"Shangri-la," Nick agreed, her enchanted smile sending his heart into a flip-flop.

She stood up in the stirrups and looked around. "But nothing looks familiar. We might as well go ba—"

Carla broke off and plunked down on the saddle, shivering, when an eerie whisper drifted across the meadow. She turned and looked to the northwest. "I've had the oddest feeling all day that I should ride in that direction." She glanced at Nick, with a wry smile. "Do you think hunches are crazy?"

Loath to admit that he'd felt the hunch, too, Nick

said, "Probably, but I'm led by them all the time. Which is lucky, since I can't read directions." When both his grin and the joke fell flat, he turned Spook northwest.

After a few minutes, Carla called out, "Stop, Nick, this is too rough for the horses." She dropped the reins over Molly's neck and ran both hands through her sweaty hair, standing the bangs up straight. "This was a dumb idea; that old cabin can't possibly be anywhere around here."

Nick unhooked a tree branch that had snagged his shirtsleeve. "I guess I'll have to give in and agree with you."

He almost fell off Spook when Carla gave a hearty yelp, startling the horses into leaping forward. "What is it? What's the matter?!" he demanded, his heart surging with adrenaline.

"Someone touched my shoulder!"

Whipping around, they both stared behind her. There wasn't a soul in sight.

And there it was—the cabin, tucked in a grove of majestic pines, mid-hillside, overlooking the creek. The roof and stone chimney had collapsed, but the log walls were intact. "How weird!" Carla said, staring at it with disbelief. Then she clasped her hands under her chin, reins dangling from her fingers. "Oh, Nick, do you suppose it really is Pierre's cabin?"

He rasped his knuckles against his jaw, staring at it with hungry, wishful eyes. Then he shook his head, leery, as always, of disappointment. "Nah, coincidences like that only happen in fiction. Hundreds of woodsmen must have built cabins in this valley, so the probability of this being *the* one is infinitesimal. Besides, there wouldn't be that much left of it after a hundred years."

"Let's have a look anyway." Slinging one tall, shiny boot over Molly's withers, Carla jumped down and tied the mare to a sapling at the edge of a patch of grassy meadow.

Nick slid off and tied Spook, then followed her into the silent, cathedrallike atmosphere under the towering pines. "I suppose maybe they did build these things to last," he said, slapping a couple of the hand-hewn logs, their corners notched precisely together. Pulling his brows down, he kicked at the stone doorstep and looked through the gaping entry, crooked from settling.

A ray of sunshine had forced its way through the dense trees, touching down inside the cabin. Suddenly a sense of such melancholy familiarity crept over Nick that he wanted to cry. Whispers seemed to call out to him.

His heart accelerated from eighty to two hundred in a millisecond when a hand slipped into his from behind and he heard a whisper louder than the others: "Déjà vu."

"*What?!*" He whirled around, and his knees went weak with relief when he saw it was Carla.

"I didn't mean to startle you," she said, giving a nervous laugh. "But I felt such an odd sensation that I'd seen you standing here before. It scared me."

"Whatever you're thinking is ridiculous!"

"I wasn't thinking anything—what were you thinking?"

"Nothing," he said sheepishly.

"Then let's go inside."

Nick swallowed audibly. "Might as well, I suppose, since we're here." Or rather, because he didn't want her to guess how chickenhearted he felt.

It didn't help when Pip, always the first, planted himself outside the door and refused to join his humans in stepping over the flat stone slab of a doorstep into the cabin.

The single room was carpeted with musty, rotten rubble and overgrown with brush, blooming wildflowers, and even a spindly sapling, anemic in the shade of the pines. A crude stone fireplace covered most of the far wall. With budding excitement, Nick

glanced at Carla. "You don't suppose there's a re-
mote chance I could dig around and find some proof
Pierre once lived here?"

"Maybe." Her violet eyes sparkled. "But be careful
you don't stir up something that's been slumbering
all these years."

"Thanks a lot; just what I wanted to hear," Nick
muttered, and began kicking cautiously through the
debris, frightening a few mice and turning up the
stash of a pack rat.

Carla watched, thinking how naturally Nick, with
his black hair and eyes and rugged body, fit into the
primitive cabin—especially when she pictured him
as she'd first seen him, in a buckskin shirt, beard,
and long hair. The cabin came alive with her little
fancy. Above the missing roof moaning pines waved
to and fro, disturbed by echoes of laughter and
weeping. A longing filled her, transcending anything
she'd ever felt before.

Frightened by the sensation, she blurted out, "How
odd to think people once struggled to make a life
here. They must have loved and given birth, laughed
and quarreled, dreamed and hoped, suffered and
died. Now there's not a trace left."

Her voice sounded loud in the silence. Nick glanced
around. The single ray of sunlight had blazed her
hair to gold . . . reminding him, somehow, of something precious he'd lost eons ago. When she moved,
her hair burned dark again. "There are puh*lenty* of
traces. I wouldn't laugh if someone suggested there
were ghosts in here," he said.

"I *wish* you hadn't said that!" She traversed the
debris to his side and linked her arm through his in
a stranglehold. "I've been trying to convince myself it
was my imagination."

"Collective imagination for two. What say we get
out of here?"

Outside in the untainted, fresh air, they both
sighed, then laughed at their fears. Pip was so happy

they'd come out safely, he even licked Nick. "Good grief, don't tell me the beast sensed something too!" Nick exclaimed, wiping his hand on his pants leg.

Carla squared her shoulders and announced, "I have a strong feeling that Michel and Emily once walked right here in this grove."

"Nah, not likely," Nick said. "If Pierre had realized that little affair was going on, he would have been as opposed as her father. He knew Michel would suffer because of it. They would have stayed away from here." He cleared his throat. "Not that I'm convinced this is Pierre's cabin, mind you."

Carla gazed at him. "How sad they couldn't stay together. Michel obviously made some kind of marriage, or you wouldn't be here. But poor, lonely Emily."

A soft wailing drifted around the grove. Nick glanced up at the swaying pine branches. "Those things make the funniest noises—almost human."

"Yes, they do." Carla looked up too. "Either that, or I'm having starvation delusions. I didn't eat any breakfast."

He brightened. "That's it—I didn't either! I'll bet that explains things. And, it's a problem easily remedied: I rustled a little something up and brought it in Spook's saddlebags. Do you want to eat here, or go find somewhere more cheerful?"

She glanced around; it was a little past midday, and the sun was high and bright, nudging down through the pines. "Let's stay here—it's peaceful and as beautiful as a park. Besides, you haven't finished your archaeological dig, so we can't leave yet."

"Mmmm," Nick said, not especially eager to brave the cabin again.

He brought the horses and tethered them. The two large, warm bodies added immensely to the life awakening in the grove around the cabin. After spreading a blanket over the carpet of pine needles, he opened the saddelbags to display deli sandwiches, an assortment of fruit, trail mix, and several cans of beer.

"My, my, a feast fit for a queen," Carla said.

"So have a throne, your highness." He bowed her onto a log, watching her curvaceous body bend, stretching the tight breeches. "No golden plates, I'm sorry to say." He held out a plastic-bagged sandwich. "You'll have to make do with your royal fingers."

"How plebeian." Pointing her upturned nose toward the sky, Carla accepted the sandwich with an extended pinky. Then she laughed. "I don't see any junk food, so I take it you're educating my eating habits."

"I wouldn't exactly call beer health food. Want one, queen o' mine?"

"Dying for one! Pull my tab, peon."

Nick sat down on the log beside her, hooked a finger in a can, and pulled. "Aa-ugh!" he roared when a frothy geyser showered him. He'd forgotten that the beer had been bouncing around on Spook's back all morning.

Jumping up, he held the spouting can at arm's length, showering Carla too. She leaped up, fell over the log, and lay on her back, howling with laughter.

"Very hilarious; go ahead and laugh." Pitching the can into the pines, he held his dripping arms out from his sides, his dignity puddling around his feet. "Funny as hell."

Echoes tinkled merrily around the trees and cabin when she went off into another gale, her booted legs kicking over the top of the log.

Giving a roar, Nick pounced, straddling her with a knee on either side of her waist and holding her wrists down above her head. "The peasants are uprising, funny girl, so prepare yourself for a beery kiss." He puckered up and began descending, dripping on her face.

She stopped his descent and sent his toes into spasm by curling her tongue and seductively licking droplets off her upper lip, laughter bubbling in her eyes.

"You're asking for it."

"Oh, no, not a fate worse than death!"

Pip picked that inopportune moment to remember his duties as protector. Wedging his head between them, he lifted a lip at Nick and snarled. "Get out of here, you dumb dog," Carla cried. "I don't want a bodyguard any longer—you're fired."

Giving them an offended look, the heeler walked away and flopped down by Spook.

"Well, hoo-ray, I've been released from executioner's row!" Nick laughed, gazing into Carla's elfin face. "Though you may have been wise to hang on to your protection. I'm only a poor, weak male, you know, and temptation is sorely tempting me."

She grinned up at him. "I'm tempted, too, and not an iota stronger than you."

"Sounds interesting," he murmured, his body rising to the occasion. "Should we test ourselves and see who's the weakest?"

Her gaze turned hot. "You're really into research, aren't you?"

"Yup." Curving himself down over her body, Nick covered her mouth with his and nibbled the satiny pinkness of her lips.

But when her tongue came out to meet his, his body exploded with need. He wanted her with a frenzy he could barely contain. Filling her mouth with his tongue, flicking, tasting, he moved the hard, aching pleasure in his groin slowly against the softness of her belly. Lifting his head, he looked down into her face. "Sweetheart . . . ?"

She smiled up at him, face flushed, lips swollen with desire. Pulling one of her hands free, she touched a finger to the dimple in his chin. "Nicky . . . ?"

"'Nicky'!" Heat lit his face. "Does that mean you're feeling warm and cozy and pliable?"

"It means I'm going crazy to make . . . uh . . . whoopee."

"What happened to one day at a time?" he asked, his voice raspy.

"Today's the day," she whispered, her voice just as husky.

That they were here, at this point, seemed so momentous, it frightened him a little. "Are you sure you won't regret it when sanity returns?"

She touched her finger to his nose and smiled up at him. "No, never. It feels so right for us to make love right here, right now, at this moment. I've never been so sure of anything in my life! I want you to show me magic."

"Well, lady, now you've gone and done it. You've touched off the fuse in this weak, human male." Laughing softly, he cupped his hands around her tantalizing mounds, their rigid tips pressing up against her delicate pink blouse.

"Oh, Nick, please," she whispered, fumbling at the buttons. "I want to feel you touch my skin."

"Let me, sweetheart; I've waited so long for this." He undid each button and brushed the sides of her blouse away from her breasts: two perfect, lovely globes. Cradling them, his fingers looked very dark against her white skin. "You're so beautiful," he whispered, awed. He bent forward, took one rosy-brown bud into his mouth, and rolled it with his tongue, then did the same to the other, until she was squirming under him. "Oh . . . oh, I think I'm going to die of want."

Moaning, she ran trembling hands over the span of his shoulders, down his long, lean back, and around to open the buttons of his shirt. She plunged her fingers into the curly black hair on his chest and began to tickle his nipples erect. "You're driving me wild, sweetheart," he said with a groan.

Carla smiled. "Show me *how* wild, Nicky."

Struggling to his feet, he pulled her upright by the

hands and led her to the blanket. After pushing the saddlebags and sandwiches haphazardly aside, he gazed at her, his grin heated and cocky. "What do you want, sweetheart?"

Wetting parted lips with her tongue, she gazed with limpid eyes at the erection pressing against his fly. Then she stepped forward and put her hands around the raging tumult. "I want you to be mine."

His eyes as limpid as hers, Nick moved his hand against her intimately. "You've been mine since the beginning of time. . . . You'll be there till the end."

His whisper had been so low, she almost hadn't heard him. And although she knew he was only embellishing his seduction with the heat of passion, the words crept into her heart all the same. She could even hear echoes of them rebounding around the grove of pines. Whispers . . . of joy.

Her lips felt swollen and numb with desire when she laughed softly. "I don't know about the beginning or end of time. All I know is, if you don't quit dragging your heels, camera bum, you'll end up ravaged."

"Whoo, that sounds scary." He slipped her blouse off, dropping it on the blanket. Then he sat her down on the log and pulled off first one boot and then the other. She stood up and endured the delicious torment of his hands peeling the clinging material of her breeches down her legs.

Standing before him in nothing but a scanty lavender bikini, she offered herself without embarrassment to his dark, heated gaze. It seemed so very, very right to be with him like this. Her breathing tripped all over itself when he lowered her to the blanket and knelt beside her to slip off the patch of lace between her legs. Sensations flooded her as he invaded every dimple and crease of her body with fingers and lips.

"I want to see you, too, Nicky," she whispered, her hands fluttering over him. "Take off your clothes."

Trembling with passion, he stripped and stood

before her, hands on hips. His body was smooth, hot with desire, hard and sculptured. A powerful love machine.

"Which reminds me . . ." she whispered, and rolled over to take a tiny packet out of a pocket in her breeches. She lifted her brows inquiringly at him. "Uh . . . ?"

"You had ideas a long time before you let me know about it, didn't you?" Grinning, he bent over and pulled a similar packet out of his pants pocket. "Yours or mine?"

Tossing hers aside, she reached up and took his. "Let me do it . . . I've waited so long for you. Come on down, I want to touch you."

He lay beside her, laughing. "I'm your obedient slave, your majesty. Do what you will with me."

"I should hope!" She ran her fingertips down over his chest and stomach and up the throbbing, satiny staff she wanted so badly. Half the titillation in the fumbling, she managed to sheathe him. Reveling in her power to drive him wild, she ran hands and kisses over his body until he groaned. "My sweet Carla, let me take you now."

"Yes, yes . . . now."

Kneeling between her spread legs, he let himself down on top of her, then lifted up onto his elbows to watch her face as he entered. "You feel so good, so good." He moaned softly, scattering hot, wet kisses up her neck. "I want to make you as happy as I am. Tell me what you want."

"Nicky, I want . . ."

Her coherency ended when he began moving. Grasping his shoulders, she wrapped her legs around his body, crying out as his strokes became harder and faster. She reached the heights, almost unable to bear the ecstasy of climax. And then it began again; he stimulated her until she cried out in so intense a release that she lost all sense of reality. Vaguely she felt Nick arch himself against her, heard him say her name, over and over until the sound faded away.

Drifting as if coming out of a trance, she heard sighing, cries, tinkling laughter tumbling around the clearing, dancing in the boughs. She felt herself floating about in the vagrant breeze whipping the tops of the pines, becoming one with the excited whispers; echoes of another time, another place. Her soul was filled with joy, but she had the oddest feeling it wasn't all her own.

The sensation disappeared when Carla opened her eyes. Drawing in a sigh that seemed to come from her toes, she murmured, "Never, ever have I felt like this before. I'm utterly emptied inside."

"Uh-huh; me too," Nick whispered, his voice deep and breathless. "And the emptied cup runneth over with . . ." He let the thought fade without expression. Lifting himself off, he curled an arm around her and rested his lips against her forehead. "It's never been like this for me either—not ever, sweetheart."

Her cup ran over in the form of tears. "I guess that's what happens when people play around with that old black magic, and fate on top of it."

He nuzzled his face in her short hair and then brushed a line of kisses from her collarbone to her chin, sighing deeply. "I knew we'd be fiery together."

Her fingers playing with the hair on his chest, Carla frowned thoughtfully. "I guess that's why it was so scary for me to go into this. Are you sorry I made you wait so long and waste precious time?"

"Uh-*uh*. You were right when you said this was the exact right time and the exact right place for our love to begin. I don't know why, but it is."

They shared a sigh, and nebulous whispers in the trees echoed it. To Carla, they sounded for all the world like voices as she gazed up into the wafting branches. Lifting her head, she looked at the broken cabin, with its blind window hole and gaping door, then dropped back down. "Nick, you don't actually believe in ghosts, do you?"

He was more interested in fitting his large, tanned hand to the curve of her small, fair waist. "Let me put it this way: If the ghosts of Michel and Emily were around, think how delighted they'd be to have someone make . . . uh . . . whoopie on their old stamping grounds."

"Oh, thanks a lot! I wish I hadn't asked." She couldn't stop herself from glancing at the cabin again. Nothing there. Still. . . . Grabbing the nearest article of clothing, she flapped Nick's shirt out over her body.

He lifted his head. "What are you doing?"

"You don't expect me to lie here in the buff after you suggested we might have an audience, do you?"

Dropping his head back on the blanket, Nick let go with that laugh of his. "I hate to disillusion you, but I'm fairly certain ghosts can see through cloth."

"You fink!" Snaking an arm out from under the shirt, she began gathering in her scattered clothes.

"Aw, sweetheart, you know damn well there's no such thing as ghosts," Nick said, running his hand up over her body from thigh to shoulder. "Come on back and cuddle in my arms."

"Maybe *I* know there aren't, but my skin doesn't—it's crawling."

Under cover of the shirt, Carla pulled on her panties, slipped her arms into her blouse, then heaved and strained, skinning her breeches up over her hips. Emerging from under the shirt, she sat on the log and lifted each leg in turn, pulling on her boots. "Hey, camera bum, I'm hungry now. All that huffin', puffin' exercise associated with sex gave me a tremendous appetite. Didn't it you?"

"No, it made me too lazy to move," Nick answered, lying on his side with his back toward her, his wavy black hair sticking out in every sweaty direction.

Grinning, she took aim with a pine cone and hit

deadeye on one of his shapely buns. "Come on, I'll bet you're dying for another beer."

He came up with a roar, sending her running, pealing laughter. "I'll give you beer, you wicked, cruel woman!"

They feasted hungrily, washing the sandwiches and trail mix down with beer, which had been subdued by the passage of time. Then, replete, they sat on the log, side by side, shadows lengthening in the grove as the sun dropped toward the west. "What an eerie atmosphere," Carla said, glancing around. "Maybe I don't believe in ghosts, but I could be persuaded that traces remain."

Smiling, Nick put his arm around her. "I think I'll restore the cabin—rebuild it into a historical monument."

"In honor of Pierre?"

"No, in honor of our first lovemaking."

Touched, Carla leaned her head on his shoulder. "Are you turning sentimental on me, camera bum?"

His dark eyes were full of laughter and warmth. "Damn right—making love to you is special enough for a memorial the size of the Washington Monument."

"Mmm, a world-class phallic symbol. Sounds more like in honor of you."

"You're asking for it, lady," he said, curving talon-like fingers at her.

She put a hand in his talons. "You said that once before, and I liked what you gave me. Unfortunately, it's getting late, and I wouldn't be caught dead in this grove after dark."

The sun had set and it was almost dark by the time they'd rubbed down the horses, fed them a measure of oats, and put them out to pasture. "Want to go out to dinner?" Nick asked, closing the gate.

Carla rubbed her behind and shook her head. "I'm

stiff and saddle-sore. All I want is to shower to wash off the beer, and then to drop in bed."

Nick shoved his hands in his pockets and braced one pointed cowboy boot on the lower rail of the fence, frowning in deep thought. After a bit he said, "There's a shower and a bed in the jockey house too."

Carla glanced at him. "You wouldn't be suggesting I stay the night, would you?"

"Well, yeah, the night"—he swallowed audibly— "or for the duration of the shoot, if you're interested."

The tentative, cautious overture was a surprise, and she studied his face, searching for . . . she didn't know what. Depth of feeling, a declaration of . . . ? But his expression was unreadable. "Better be careful, camera bum, you're brushing dangerously close to commitment. You haven't forgotten you're a ramblin' kind of guy, have you?"

"No, but you've pushed me into extraordinary measures," he said, hiding whatever feelings he might have had with a grin. "You were so hard to get close to, I'm scared you'll back out again. I want to keep you right next to me, where I can keep an eye on you. If you're worried about the state of the house, I swept out the mouse droppings and furnished it adequately from secondhand stores and the auctions. It may not be elegant, but it's comfy enough."

Leaning back against the fence beside him, Carla gazed at the little house, barely visible in the dusk. Her system ran rampant with mixed feelings. It excited her to think of spending several intimate weeks with Nick—"for the duration," as he'd put it. But if she got too close, how could she bear to let him go at the end?

"I'm really tempted, Nick, but I have to think this over. I'm not sure I'm ready to move in and play house yet." Going up on her toes, she kissed him lightly on the lips. "And neither are you, camera bum."

He sighed deeply, as if he'd felt anxious and ambivalent about his offer also. "Well, if you won't move in, why don't you at lest let me fix you a royal dinner at my place, your majesty?"

"Now that's something I can handle, peon," she said, her eyes gleaming. "It'd tickle my little old breeches off to have dinner at your place."

"I was counting on it," he murmured.

Laughing, they walked hand in hand down the dusky path toward the jockey house.

Seven

The fantasy running through Nick's head as they walked toward the jockey house was snuffed out like a candle flame when he came around the corner and saw Bunny sitting on the porch. Her spandex biker's tights glowed fluorescent green in the fading sunset. Her bicycle was leaning against the railing. "Where have you been?!" she demanded, hopping off the porch and rushing forward.

He could hear the agitated snapping of her gum from yards away. "Why, what's up?"

Pip rushed at her with a threatening growl. "Oh, aren't you the cutest little snookums," she cooed, cradling the fanged muzzle in her hands. To Nick's disgust, the bloodthirsty beast melted into a fawning pool of gray fur at her feet. "Good grief, you both reek of beer—what *have* you been doing?" Wrinkling her nose, she flashed a brilliant smile. "Hi, you must be Carla, nice to meet you." Her smile blinked off. "Nick, Juan Fernandez located the Amazon rain forest Indians you've been hoping to film."

A rocket of excitement drove everything else out of his mind. "Juan found them! When?"

"Several days ago, so you better get a move on if you want to connect. You can't get anywhere out of

Missoula this late in the day, so Pres okayed his pilot to fly you to Salt Lake City in the Learjet to catch a red-eye to LAX, then hop to Brazil first thing in the morning. Hurry up and change clothes. I already packed your safari duds, some clean jocks, and crated your field cameras."

"What *is* this about Amazon Indians?" Carla exclaimed, trying to hide her disappointment. "I thought you were vital to the making of this movie."

"He already did his part; now Pres and I can handle the rest," Bunny said. "This is a hundred times more important than that damn movie. So get a move on, will you?!"

Ignoring her, Nick ran his fingers through his hair, gazing at Carla. Any other time his system would have been revving with the thrill of adventure, but now he felt torn. "God, what miserable timing," he said. "You're a hell of a lot more important to me than the damn movie. But Bunny is right: I can't drop this opportunity—I've been trying to film these Indians for two years."

Carla gave his arm a little shake. "It's okay—I'll take a rain check on the dinner and . . . uh . . . whatever. We've been going at everything too fast anyhow, and this'll be a good opportunity for us to stand back and think things out. I'll run up to the ranch house and get out of your way."

"Oh, no you don't," he said, grabbing her wrist. "Come inside; I want to explain where I have to go and why."

Bunny flapped her hands at them. "Oh, for gosh sake, go listen to him, or he'll stand around arguing for the rest of the night." She sat down on a rocking chair, Pip's worshipful head on her knee. "But make it a chop-chop good-bye."

Nick took Carla's arm and quick-stepped her in the door and through the house. Down the hallway, he steered her into a bedroom he used for an office, workshop, and studio. There were several still and movie cameras sitting around, along with tape players and recorders. A computer on a desk was surrounded by a scatter of yellow-highlighted letters.

"Here, look at this." He waved to the photos of jungles, fires and devastation, and banana and coffee plantations pinned to a cork-covered wall. "They're burning the rain forest in South America." Then he touched three hazy snaps of a few pathetic natives. "Two years ago the Smithsonian contracted me to do a film of these South American Indians. They're Stone Age primitive and live off what they can kill with poisoned darts. A big-game hunter, Juan Fernandez, sometimes makes contact with them, but they've never let me get close enough to film."

She nodded, frowning intently at the pictures. "They look half-starved."

"Yeah, the tribe has shrunk to only about thirty since civilization began encroaching on their territory, bringing in diseases."

Carla glanced at him. "So your video documentary will preserve their way of life for posterity, in case they're pushed into extinction."

Nick nodded, surprised by her insight; he hadn't expected her to understand. "*If* I can catch up to them." He made a wry face. "And if they don't use me for a poison-dart pincushion first."

"That's not funny!" she exclaimed, her face tensing. "I didn't think about you being in danger."

"I won't be—" Nick broke off, reminding himself to be open and honest. "Well, a little, maybe. These Indians are as capricious as hell and very mistrustful. What bothers me more is this might be a false alarm, like all the other times. So far, the closest I've come is a glimpse before they disappear. There's nothing I hate more than failing and being disappointed."

Carla smiled and touched his cheek with her fingertips. "Then you'd better get going, shouldn't you?"

The idea of leaving her turned Nick to jelly inside. "I don't feel so eager to do this rain forest thing any longer," he said, gathering her into his arms. "I wouldn't have gotten into it if I'd known I was going to meet you."

Clasping her arms around his neck, she smiled. "Yes you would have—it's your job."

Bunny's voice rang through the house. "Nick, will you hurry it up?!"

"Yeah, in a minute!" he bellowed, and tightened his arms around Carla. "If I go, will you welcome me back?"

"Sure, I'll shoot up the rockets and raise the flags."

"Good," he whispered. "Hey, think about moving in with me when I come back, okay? We'll have precious little time left, and it'd be a shame to waste a minute of it."

Carla cupped her hands around the raspy shadow of evening beard on his jaws. "Why don't you think about us just having a nice little late-summer affair after you come back? No ties, no demands, no expectations."

Another first: In all his other romantic encounters he'd been the one saying that. Now he felt hurt. "Is that what you really want?"

"I told you what I want if I let myself get *involved* again, camera bum. The world, the universe, and . . . you for a forever man." She laughed softly. "Are you ready to give me that?"

Nick creased his brow and bit into his upper lip, then gave a laugh. "Woof, you ask hard questions."

She nodded. "Speaking for myself, it'd hurt too much to let you go in the end if we get in too deep. But we're both experienced adults, so we ought to be able to survive a simple, uncluttered affair."

She clapped her palms on his cheeks before he could think of an argument. "Quit quibbling and go take a shower. They'll never let you on the plane smelling like a keg of beer."

• • •

Carla thought she and Bunny must have made quite a pair standing at the small Hamilton airport, one in an English riding outfit, the other in a fluorescent biker's second skin. They watched the Learjet scream down the runaway, lift off, and swoop eastward toward the moon rising over the mountains. Red and green lights blinked as the plane carried Nick southward to Salt Lake City and away.

Bunny snapped her gum with satisfaction. "Well, that's that; he should make it."

Carla felt more empty inside than satisfied. "How long do you suppose he'll be gone?"

"Depends—if he can't make contact, he'll be back in days. If they let him get close enough, he'll probably be gone a few months."

"Months . . . ?" Carla's heart sank. There were less than three months to the end of his lease. It surprised her to feel tears rise in her eyes, and she quickly walked toward her car to hide them.

Bunny kept pace, studying her curiously. "In Nick's business, he has to grab when opportunity knocks."

"I *know* that!" Carla climbed into the driver's seat.

Bunny slouched in the passenger's side, one knee braced on the dash. "Just thought I'd mention it, because you look like a nice sort, and I'd hate to see you start expecting too much."

The green-eyed demon reared its ugly head as Carla drove up the road. She glanced at the lovely young woman and couldn't stop herself from asking, "Are you in love with Nick?"

"Honey, I'm having an affair with my computer. Unlike men, it always does exactly what I want, it's always there when I need it, and it might even be a little smarter than I am."

Carla laughed. "That makes better sense than anything I've heard today."

Bunny glanced sideways. "Are *you* in love with him?"

The frank question hit her in the face like ice water. "Good grief, no! I don't think so—I hardly even know the man. We just . . . well . . . I sure hope not."

Bunny snapped her gum contemplatively, then popped a bubble. "Do you know much about Nick and his dyslexia?"

"No, not really. Do you?"

"I'm full of useless information. It's more common in boys with above-average intelligence. It's a case of the mind working fine, but the shuttle to the outside is derailed or traveling a random route. Thomas Edison was one, Albert Einstein, Leonardo da Vinci, Cher—so Nick's in good company. In the most severe cases, the kid is never able to learn to read, like Nick. Some can't spell, some can't express themselves. Some have no coordination and trip all over everything. Whichever, it devours self-esteem."

"Yes, I'm sure it does." Carla turned her car under the big white arch over the Hudson driveway. "It's amazing he was able to become such a successful, confident man."

"Successful, yes." Another bubble; a pop. "Now comes the unforgivable part I've been leading up to. I like the guy and I've got to say it—don't hurt him, okay?"

Carla parked the car behind the house and tightened her fists on the steering wheel. "I doubt it'll be Nick left behind crying when everything comes to an end."

Bunny hopped out and leaned down to look through the window. "I wouldn't take bets on that. Big macho has a tender skin."

Giving a jaunty wave, she ran across the yard to retrieve her bike and pedal back in darkness to Little Hollywood.

Carla went upstairs in the ranch house and showered the saddle-stiffness out and the beer off, put on a nightie, and fell into bed, utterly exhausted. But she couldn't sleep.

Her mind was filled with the sweet rovin' man who had brought her to exquisite life. Touching her lips and breasts, she smiled over a memory of Nick's marvelous, cocky face and relived the excitement of his body on hers.

Then came worry over his being in danger. Uncertainty over if and when he'd return. Dread, because she hated thinking that the restless, dynamic life she so loved about Nick would also eventually take him away from her for good.

In the wee hours of the morning, she imagined whispers of sadness and weeping drifted in through her open window. For some reason they brought Emily to mind. Had Emily considered her short period of magic with Michel worth the loneliness she'd suffered for the rest of her life?

She thought about it a minute, then glanced at the window, remembering the whispers in the boughs at the cabin. Emily wasn't suffering the loneliness far, far beyond her lifetime—was she?

Carla already felt lonely, and Nick hadn't been gone a day.

The first Thursday in September was the guys' bowling night, so the "girls" gathered at Hudson's Hair to gossip and unwind before going home. Carla was sitting at the desk, her mind off in Never-Never Land with Nick. Over and over, she circled the date on her account book with her pen—he'd been gone twelve days. Twelve long, lonely days, and she hadn't heard a word from him. She'd discovered it was true—absence *did* make the heart grow fonder. Very, very fond. It almost seemed as if she'd fallen in—

She jumped and looked up when a balled candy

wrapper bounced on the account book lying open in front of her.

"Who you woolgathering with?" Bonnie asked, slouched comfortably in a styling chair.

"No one, I'm simply very engrossed in paying bills," she said, lifting an envelope to lick the flap shut.

"Well, I haven't seen your hand move that pen for the last ten minutes, and I've asked you the same question three times. I asked, what is this disgusting thing you have in a vase here at your station? Do you want me to throw it out?"

"Don't you dare touch that!" Carla leaped up and ran across the salon to save the white rose, now a dry, brown nugget. Stowing it safely, she hitched her hip up on the edge of the desk and braced herself for flak.

Bonnie didn't disappoint her; she glanced around at the young women lounging in the other styling chairs and asked, "Did you see that sprint to save a piece of garbage? Tell me, does our Carla act like she might have something going on with—let's see if my memory serves—a black-haired, black-eyed, brassy, bold fella?"

A chorus of "uh-huhs" rang out.

She bit her lip to fight back an incriminating grin. "Would I be hanging around with you jokers if I had anything going on?"

"Jill's Ralph is working out at your place, remember?" Gayle volunteered. "He told my Cass a while back that he saw you take off with Nick Leclerc on horses, dressed in the fanciest riding clothes he ever saw. Did he mention it to you, Jill?" Gayle asked.

Jill was sitting in a corner, making nervous folds in her denim skirt. She shook her head.

Carla grinned. "I thought Ralph was working for the movie company, not the FBI."

"And what about the sudden change in your appearance? Seems to me I remember you in jeans and blouses only a month ago. Don't tell me you jumped into *that* outfit for us jokers."

"This little old thing?" Carla straightened her tight black miniskirt and oversized floral top, jerking up the neckline, which had fallen off one shoulder. She wasn't about to admit she'd begun dressing with an eye toward Nick coming back unexpectedly. "I'm in the business of style and beauty, so I decided it was about time I dressed the part."

"But that doesn't explain your hollow-eyed, spacey look, which exactly resembles a woman in the throes," Gayle said, lifting her soda can for a sip. "Just remember, our shoulders are available if things go sour."

Carla sighed. Maybe it would help to voice her worries openly to these, her closest friends. "How am I supposed to know if things are going sour? They were barely starting when Nick disappeared into the Amazon rain forest to film some Indians. He's been there almost two weeks."

"What's he doing *there*? Isn't he making a movie?"

"No, what he's doing now is far more important than a movie." She got up and paced the squeaky floor as she explained his project.

Bonnie quirked a corner of her mouth. "Men! Just when you'd like to rake 'em over the coals good, they go on out and do something commendable!"

Jill spoke for the first time, her voice teary. "Are you in love with him?"

Carla sighed deeply. "I don't know. All I know is I can't quit thinking about him, and I'm a heck of a lot more miserable than I was before he happened upon the scene. If that's love, I'm not crazy about it."

"Sounds like the real thing, all right."

"So, is there a marriage in the offing?" Bonnie asked.

Carla picked up the vase and fingered the dry, brown rose, then shook her head. "Even if this should turn out to be love, and even if Nick were the marrying type, which he isn't, he isn't a Bitterroot Valley kind of guy. And I'd never consider going anywhere near Hollywood, even for him."

Tears filled Jill's eyes and she daubed her nose with a tissue. "If you loved him, wouldn't you put up with anything or go anywhere to be with him?"

Carla cocked her head, amused that Jill was so sentimental over her hypothetical romantic dilemma. "I doubt that it would be a very healthy relationship if I gave up being a person in my own right. The relationship would be doomed from square one."

Jill thought about that for a moment. "Maybe he'll stay here with you when he gets this runnin' around out of his system."

"Then he'd give up being a person in *his* own right. This isn't something to be gotten out of his system— ramblin' *is* Nick. Not even Bunny can predict where he'll go, when, or for how long."

Gayle lifted her brows. "Do you actually trust that Hollywood goddess around your man?"

"Sure, Bunny's all right," Carla said, and added with a laugh, "as long as Nick doesn't come back reincarnated as a computer."

The girls detoured into a siege of catty gossip. "Have you ever seen so many trendy, *skinny*, gorgeous women in your life since that filming company came into the valley?" Bonnie declared. "Lordy, I wouldn't even trust my Jackson around those females, and he's too shy to flirt."

"Did anyone see the guy with great big holes designed into his jeans, all up the legs from ankles to fly—even the rear, with his boxer shorts sticking out? My, did that make my heart go pitty-pat."

"He's probably gay."

"How about the woman with a tattoo of a man's hand grabbing her left breast?"

A chorus of scandalized "no-o-os" arose. "My hubby better not try fitting his hand into that picture!"

When Jill began sobbing, the laughter shut off as if a button had been turned.

Belatedly, Carla realized it wasn't *her* dilemma the young woman had been sniffling over. She went to the back of the salon to kneel at her side. "What's wrong, honey?"

"Ralph is seeing one of those fancy girls." Jill's voice rose to a squeak, and she burst into fresh sobbing.

Carla grabbed a towel to sop her tears. "Are you sure? Have you talked to him about it?"

"He just gets mad and calls me a naggy wife. *He* says he's workin' things so he can become an actor. But *I* found lipstick on his shirts when I did the washing, and a long red hair in his undershorts."

They all looked at Jill's head of dark brown hair as she wiped her face. "And I think there's more to it than a woman. I think he's been trying things out. His eyes look real funny sometimes when he comes home. I'm so worried." She buried her face in the towel and sobbed.

The implications were clear to Carla: sex and drugs. Memories of her sister flooded back. Clasping her arms over her middle, she began striding around the room. "I knew something like this would happen! *Why* didn't I work harder to keep that movie company out of the valley?"

Her anger exploded. "Somebody lock up the shop when you leave. I'm going out to the ranch and see Preston Mann. I'll straighten this thing out."

Carla drove her car up the lane to Nick's end of the ranch. It was the first time she'd ventured near Little Hollywood. Other than the three huge semitrailers full of props and equipment, the rest of the encampment looked much like any other trailer park, dwarfed by the mountains just beyond. RVs were parked in a rough circle around a makeshift plaza, and there were even some tents.

Filming had ended with the passing of good light, and the day's-end activity seemed perfectly normal. Children sang and jumped rope, a couple of poodles yapped, women in folding chairs gossiped, several people tossed a ball around in a field, a courting couple smooched.

Someone directed Carla to Preston Mann's RV. She knocked, her mouth set.

He surprised her by catching her up in an exuberant hug as soon as he opened the door. "Carla Hudson, but it's so wonderful to see you again! You look *marvelous*. Why on earth did you decide to bury yourself in this godforsaken valley? We miss you in the business."

Carla extricated herself, laughing. "Go on, Pres, we both know I was just one of the faceless troops."

"*I* miss you. Don't you miss us a little bit? Come on back to work—I need every talented hand I can get."

She fought an unnerving surge of nostalgia. "I'd be lying if I said I didn't miss the life sometimes, but I'd never go back."

"A shame, but come in and sit down in my skimpy dinette. Lord, I can't wait to finish the shoot so I can go back and live in a real house again. Should have the film in the can within two weeks. How about I break out a bottle of bubbly in honor of the occasion?"

"Two weeks! It went so fast." Carla sat on a chair, her heart dropping; what if Nick didn't get back before the end? Would she ever see him again?"

"Didn't seem fast to me," Pres said, taking a bottle out of the dinky fridge. "Not when I don't have a fig of control over the weather, the light, or those temperamental creative personalities. Not to mention that the Indians live on a time schedule of their own, which has nothing to do with clocks."

The nostalgia grew stronger. "Where are you in it?"

"We've managed to film the young lovers rolling naked in the pine needless, pledging their undying love, but we haven't done their initial meeting yet." He popped the cork and poured wine. "Romantic old fool that I am, I'm saving the breakup scene for last. Just to be different."

Pres handed her a stemmed glass and lifted his own. "Speaking of romantic, here's to you, the lady who has sent our Nicky reeling."

She gave an embarrassed laugh. "Good grief, does everyone in the country know about my love life?"

"No, just me, because Nick and I go way back." He sat down across from her. "I met him when he came out of college with a chip the size of a log on his shoulder, determined to prove he was as capable as anyone, even if he couldn't read. He was, too; could have been one of the best movie cameramen in the business if he'd stayed with it."

"Why didn't he?" she asked, hungry to hear anything about Nick and his life.

Pres grunted. "He developed a crush on some pretty-faced starlet. Sweet as honey when she wanted something, nasty nature inside. Joked about his disability in public. Dumped him for someone who could boost her up the ladder. Left him with self-esteem the size of a peanut."

Carla pressed her hands on either side of her face, aching for him. "He didn't tell me about that."

"Stiff-necked pride. I'd begun doing environmental films and thought a wilderness assignment might purge him of his funk. It did, and he was so good at it, he went into business on his own." He slapped the table. "Nick'd scalp me if he knew I'd let my mouth flap this way."

"I'm glad you did." Carla picked up her glass and toyed with the stem, mulling over this new insight into Nick. He was so proud and defensive, her heart ached over how ridiculed and rejected he must have felt.

"But you came to talk to me about something, didn't you? Your face was a thundercloud when you came to the door."

"What . . . ? Oh, yes, I did." The brunt of her anger had softened. "A friend of mine says her husband is involved with one of your women and sampling drugs."

Preston frowned. "I can't play housemother to the women, but as for drugs, we're pretty clean. As usual we have our camp followers and groupies, so the trouble could be coming from them. I'll see what I can find out, okay?"

"If you don't, I'll ring the bell on you," Carla said, getting up to walk to the door. "It disgusts me to think of people popping things right here on our ranch."

"Understood," he answered. "I'll look into it."

Driving back down the lane toward the ranch house, Carla knew in her heart that Pres could look into it until doomsday and still wouldn't be able to stop any of the deviant behavior. She clenched her fists on the wheel of her car, feeling sick. Furious. Guilty.

Eight

Carla parked in front of the house. Pip wasn't barking his usual welcome as she climbed the steps of the
back stoop. She turned to look out over the ranch,
wondering where the pesky mutt could be.

Dusk had fallen and sunset was flaming behind
the mountains. Her breath stopped when she saw
that the windows of the jockey house were lit. "*Nick,*"
she whispered, a warm, all-invasive feeling budding
in her breast.

Heart racing, she ran down the path and up onto
the porch of the small house. She finger-combed her
hair and stepped into the living room. One mystery
was solved when she saw Pip lying on a battered
sofa, thumping his tail sheepishly.

"Traitor," she murmured, and looked curiously
around at freshly painted walls, shabby furniture, and
a new TV set. The run-down kitchen was furnished
with an old wooden dinette set, vintage appliances, a
microwave, and another TV. Following the watery
sound of a shower, she walked down the hall and
looked into Nick's bedroom. A suitcase was lying
open on the floor, clothes were thrown on the bed,
and there was another TV set. No decorative niceties
anywhere in the house.

Sitting down on the bed, she wondered if Nick knew how to make a house into a home. The unnamed emotion in her breast unfolded into a tender wish to make a cozy nest for that lonely rovin' man. Smiling, she pressed his travel-stained white shirt to her face.

The earthy spiciness of his scent sparked her body to life and sent her into the steamy bathroom. His tall, broad-shouldered form was hazily visible behind the shower curtain, arms braced on the wall, leaning his head into the spray. The emotion in Carla's breast exploded into full blossom; it seemed she might explode if she didn't touch him. Slipping out of her clothes, she stepped into the tub to wrap her arms around his waist. "Welcome home, Nicky."

"Wha-at?!" He straightened up so fast he bumped his head on the shower nozzle. "Ouch, dammit!"

"Poor baby, want me to kiss your heady all better?" Carla asked as she practiced on the sleek, wet muscles of his back.

Turning around in her arms, he crushed her against his body. "Sweetheart, Carla, oh Lord, am I glad to see you. Forget my heady—kiss me where it counts."

Before she had a chance to oblige, Nick claimed her mouth, sipping and tugging on her lips with his, invading with his tongue. The burr of his unshaven face tantalized her skin. Turning off the water, he stepped out onto the bath rug with her. "Oh, Lord, I missed you. Let me look at you and make sure you're real and not a dream."

His midnight eyes covered her body with such a blast of heat, she thought the droplets of water would boil. Taking a thick blue towel off the rack, he ministered to her face and her body, lighting fires with every touch.

She laughed softly, took the towel, and ruffled his wet hair, looking into the strength and sensitivity of his face, the humor, the cunning dimple in his chin.

"It's been building ever since I saw your lights. I've got to say it or burst."

"Sounds momentous—say what?"

"I think I love you," she whispered. It was a lighthearted avowal, and she didn't expect anything but a lighthearted "I love you too" in return from her ramblin' man. Which she wouldn't believe for a moment.

It surprised her when everything about him froze: his body and face, his breathing. Even his heartbeat seemed to stop. Then he tweaked the towel out of her hands and wrapped it around his waist as if to protect himself. "That's a highfalutin word for what happens when your juices fire up, Carla," he said, holding her at bay with his teasing. "Call it lust and enjoy it for what it is; call it love and you end up expecting too much."

He couldn't have hurt her more if he'd slapped her. Grabbing her clothes, she rushed to the door. Then a surge of anger stopped her in mid-step. *How dare he throw her love back in her face?!* Spinning around, she had her mouth open to lash out—but didn't speak a word.

Her abrupt turn caught him with an agonized, vulnerable, yearning expression on his face. Before the shutters fell again, she saw all the loneliness she'd sometimes sensed about him, clear and unmistakable in his eyes. Despite all his cocky male ego, she realized, this man was terrified of love.

Knowing he resented sympathy, she planted herself in front of him. "Nick Leclerc, I started loving you long before the juices were flowing! I'll still be loving you long after you've left and forgotten me. So don't you dare talk to me about lust!"

"Oh, there's no danger I'll ever forget you, Carla," he said quietly, crossing his arms over his chest. "Trust me—you may think you love me now, in the heat of the moment, but the novelty and the chemistry are bound to wear off. As you pointed out yourself that night in your salon."

"Don't throw my words back at me!" she said angrily, hugging her balled clothes against her chest. "I don't *think* I love you, Nick. I've *thought* I was in love before, but what I felt then was kid's play compared to this." She scowled at him. "And since you brought up the night in the salon, aren't you the one who was prattling about fate and magic lasting forever?"

He tightened his crossed arms. "I suppose I did, but I didn't think of them as lo—" He couldn't get the word out, and tried again: "Carla, I—"

Time seemed to stop. Nick stood motionless, eyes closed, biting into his upper lip. Sweat beaded his forehead as he waged a battle with himself.

Sweat broke out on her brow, too, because she knew he'd been hurt so terribly in the past by people he'd wanted to love. "Nick, I don't expect you to say anything you don't feel."

"No, that's my problem—I do feel it, and I want you to know." A moment passed, then he said almost shyly, "I love you, Carla." His shoulders went limp with a release of tension. "I. Do. Love. You." He opened his eyes and smiled. "Woof, those are hard words to get out. I hope you realize I've never said them to any other woman."

She saw that in his raw, vulnerable expression, and her heart melted in waves of tenderness. Tears of joy blinded her eyes. "Oh, Nick . . ."

"I love you," he whispered wonderingly, the words coming easier now that the barrier had been broken. He reached his hand toward her.

Shifting her clothes, she put one hand into his. With a strong, warm clasp, Nick bound her to him, making them one as solidly as any ceremony, any ring, could have. "My darling," she said in a choked voice. "Oh, I do love you so much. Truly."

He gazed at her tenderly, seriously. "Being in love

is a new wilderness for me, and I don't know what's going to come of it."

She gazed back at him. "I know."

Stepping forward, he cradled her in his arms as if she were a precious, fragile treasure, then rained kisses up and down her neck. After a moment, his breathing became irregular and his body stirred against hers. "Where do we go from here in this fascinating exploration of ours?" he whispered against her skin.

Her lips curved in an erotic smile and she pressed her nude body against him. "Why don't we go back and take up what we were doing before we got into all this love stuff."

"What a lovely idea." Nick laughed softly and took her clothes out of her arms, dropped them on the floor, then moved her slowly across the bathroom, thigh to thigh, body to body, until they were standing on the bathmat. "Is this where we left off?" he whispered, taking the towel off to caress the mounds of her breasts. What did it matter that they were already dry?

Fiery responses rushed through her body. "Oh, yes, you've got it right." Grasping his arms, Carla sucked in her breath as he toweled her thighs and the pulsing area between. Going down on his knees, he kissed that same pulsing area, touched it with his tongue, driving her insane with desire, "Did you miss me?" he asked, and smiled up at her.

"I missed you, Nicky," she cried out. "I needed you so. Need you—oh!" Desperate to touch him, too, she dropped to her knees and buried her face in the crisp hair on his chest, tormented his nipples with her tongue. Following a black trail down over his stomach, she made love to his passion.

"Oh, baby, sweetheart," he said with a groan, holding her head. "I dreamed of this. I want you so bad. Now."

Lifting her into his arms, Nick brought her to the

bedroom and lay her on the bed. Taking the little packet out of a drawer, he gave a cocky grin. "But one of us has a little job to do first."

"Work, work, work."

Laughing, Carla pulled him down beside her and went at the task of sheathing him with such exuberance that his words came in erratic gasps. "Whoa, you're getting better at this. Hope you haven't been practicing while I was gone."

"There'll never be anyone else, ever." Wild and wet with desire, she climbed on top and took him in, making him a part of herself. "You're the only magic I'll ever need, my darling."

Nick buried his face in her neck. "Fate . . . fate is the secret. We're meant to be here like this, and in love."

"Then take me now—make me yours," she whispered, desperately wishing it could be forever.

The rhythmic dance bonded them together in love and passion. The only whispers they heard this time were the joy and ecstasy from their own lips, and cries of a surging release. Slowly, the tremors ended and Carla dropped her head on Nick's sweaty shoulder, listening to the race of his heart under her ear. Her body lifted like a ship at sea on his every harsh breath.

After a moment, he touched his lips to her cheek and laughed softly, happily, running a finger down the curve of her neck. "I love you . . . love you . . . And I missed you so much . . . oh, so much while I was gone. Everything was so *nothing* without you."

"Me too." Lying on the sweet mattress of his angular, masculine body, Carla smiled blissfully, blanketed in their love. "I couldn't sleep or even eat while you were gone. That's how much I missed you."

"Did you really?"

Bracing her elbows against his shoulders, she looked down at him. "Really. You're the spark that gives me life."

He frowned, small muscles on either side of his jaw contracting. "I wish I could promise you everything and tell you we'll be together till the end of time. But I—"

Carla cut him off with a finger to his lips, then touched the scar on his brow. "I don't expect you to make any promises you can't keep, darling. I know who you are, and I understand why you have to do what you do."

"Maybe you know me better than I know myself, then, because I'm not so sure any longer."

Rolling off his body, she supported her head with a hand. "Now, please, tell me our separation was justified. Was your trip to the jungle successful?"

"No, it wasn't." Brows contracting, Nick blew out a breath. "The Indians seemed to accept me at first, but before I could accustom them to seeing my cameras and take one frame, they faded away in the night. Mysticism, or instinct, or something, must have told them to leave."

"You must have been sick with disappointment." Carla put her arm around him, tucking her hand between his chest and biceps. "What'll you do, give up on them?"

"No, it's too important a project to give up. Next time or the hundreth time, I'll get 'em. I have to— they're dying off too fast. Measles took seven of them while I was there." He made a sour mouth. "It was a sad trip. I needed a pat on the head when I came back, and couldn't find you for one. That's why you found me in the shower—I was trying to drown my sorrows."

Carla patted his head, then straightened the wild disarray of his hair with tender fingers. "If I'd known, I would have been right here for you."

Nick gave a heartfelt sigh. "I'm beginning to suspect I'll be mighty lonely after the movie is over and I trundle the Enterprise back home." He stared at the ceiling, forehead creased with wrinkles, and asked tentatively, "Would you ever consider going back to California?"

Agonizingly, she drew back, then sat up and hugged herself. "I won't make any promises I can't keep either, Nick. I can't go back."

He sat up, too, studying her with soul-searching dark eyes. "We've declared our love, we've had sex—we must know each other well enough for you to tell me why you can't."

Carla held herself rigid, afraid if she told him, she might start crying and never quit. She knew in her heart she had to, though, because hurting Nick would be a hundred times worse than losing control. Even so, she put it off. "Tell you what, I'll explain if you feed me. Can you cook anything besides deli sandwiches and nervous beer?"

Nick slipped into grubby clothes and went to the kitchen, leaving Carla in the shower, rinsing off the dregs of love. Humming, he looked in the fridge and unearthed a few spuds and a pickle or two, and steaks and veggies from the freezer compartment. He wasn't much of a chef, but he thought he could turn his collection into a meal with the aid of the micro-wave. Though she deserved better: ambrosia and manna from heaven.

He gladly would have sacrificed *himself* up on an altar after her warm welcome home. She gave him a sense of fulfillment he'd never experienced before; she'd infiltrated his very soul. He couldn't remember being so happy as he felt right now.

Nick's humming died when he thought about her flat refusal to consider California—not that he'd opened up like a flower in asking her to commit, he reminded himself. A niggling worry chewed his mind as he watched the steaks thaw in the microwave: Maybe Carla saw love talk as something that ma-ture, experienced adults bandied about in a summer affair. Love was pretty much new to him, and he didn't know how to trust the feeling.

Despite that, a goofy smile spread over his face when she came into the kitchen, looking achingly lovely in a miniskirt and a big-necked blouse dropped over one bare shoulder. "Hey, gorgeous, what happened to the cowgirl I came to know and—" he swallowed audibly—"love?"

"Love you, too, camera bum," she said, every bit of it glowing in her violet eyes. "And you look pretty smashing yourself."

His feet were bare and his hair was sticking up from tumbling in bed wet; his jaw was itchy with beard; he was wearing a faded red T-shirt and holey jeans. "Just a little designer something out of my closet."

"Veddy, veddy chic."

Carla nosed out two clean place mats and set the table with mismatched china and silverware. "How'd you seduce my bodyguard away?" she asked, stepping over Pip, who was lying in the middle of the floor gazing up at Nick with adoring eyes.

Nick poked at the steaks roasting on a burner-top grill. "The bloodthirsty beast started jumping all over me when I drove into the yard, and he's been stuck like glue since. Must be my irresistible charm."

She hooted. "More likely, you brought something exotic back from the jungle and hexed him into being your slave. I must have caught a whiff, too—which would explain my brazen behavior in the shower."

"Damn, you guessed." He turned away from the stove to kiss the delectable curve of her neck. "However, if you're my slave, why am I the guy doing dinner?"

"I know a hex or two of my own." Carla kissed him on the tip of each shoulder, then whispered, "There's smoke rising from the stove, vassal."

Nick dished up the meal, then sat down and leaned his elbows on the table, watching Carla eat, fascinated by her tongue flicking out, licking her lips. In lieu of dragging her back to bed again, he said, "Hey, junk-food freak, I don't see you turning up your nose at nutrition."

She glanced up and laughed. "All the . . . uh . . . exercise put me on the brink of starvation, but this really was delicious," she said, popping the last bite into her mouth.

"Want to go sit in the living room and have coffee with a wee dram of brandy in it?"

"I'd love to."

Settling Carla on the spring-sprung sofa, Nick fixed two mugs of liberally laced Swiss mocha. Sitting beside her, he put his cup on the blue box standing in for a coffee table and forced the issue she'd been avoiding: "Why can't you move back to Southern California?"

She crossed her knees, then uncrossed them. Answering filled her with dread, though if Nick hadn't brought up the subject, *she* would have. Keep it light, she told herself, no histrionics. "It's a long-drawn-out story. Kind of ugly."

He cupped his big hand around her cheek. "Most hard stories are."

Kissing his palm, Carla got up to wander around the room. She stopped to finger the buttons of the TV set, guessing that it was vital to a man who couldn't read to keep abreast of world affairs. She glanced at Nick; Pip had climbed up on the sofa and flopped down with his head on his thigh. It helped to know he had known tragedies of his own.

Jumping in willy-nilly, she said, "One of my stylists says her husband is fooling around with one of the women at the movie site and coming home with funny eyes. I told Preston Mann I won't stand for free sex and drugs on Grace's ranch. That's what this is all about, Nick."

He hitched forward to prop his elbows on his knees. "I suppose deviant behavior is bound to turn up around a shoot—goes hand in hand with creative, pressured personalties."

"Jill deserves better than having outsiders come in and booby-trap her husband."

"Assuming he's a grown man, isn't he responsible for his own actions?"

"He wouldn't have acted if he hadn't had a buffet of sex and drugs laid out before him. Inexperienced people find that sort of thing to tempting to resist." Her eyes blazed with anger. "*I* know!" She took a deep breath and stepped over the threshold. "My baby sister died of an overdose."

First Nick pinched his eyes shut and grimaced, then he got up and came toward her. "Ah, honey, I'm sorry. That's terrible."

"I haven't got to the terrible part yet." She backed away; if he touched her, she'd fly apart. Perching on the sofa, she tried to go on.

Nick boosted Pip off to the floor and sat down beside her, sensitive enough to leave space between them. "Tell me about your sister. What kind of girl was she?"

Carla clasped her hands tightly. *No histrionics.* "Janet was five years younger than me, and only three when my mother died. Dad was a set man in the movie business and gone a lot, so he brought us to stay with Grace. Then after four years, he got remarried and reunited the family. I was thirteen by the time his marriage broke up, and old enough to watch out for Janet myself."

"Must have been a heavy responsibility."

"No, I was used to it. My Mom got sick shortly after my sister was born, so I'd been mothering her all her life."

Nick clasped his hands under his chin. "And who mothered Carla?"

"No one, I guess, except Grace." To cover her chin quiver, she sipped coffee, the heat of the brandy traveling down her throat. "When school was out,

Janet and I would hang around the shoots. That's when the bug bit and hair became it for me."

"But not for Janet, I take it."

"No, she got hooked by the glitz in *front* of the camera. She was so pretty—none of this Hudson pixy face of mine—and everyone kept telling her she could out-glamour the stars. She was still a gullible country girl at heart, and swallowed every word as gospel. When she graduated from high school, she expected the pearly gates to open and angels to lift her into stardom with blaring trumpets."

Nick nodded slowly. "Old, sad story—hopefuls circling the fringes like starving kids outside a bakery window."

Carla lifted the mug, but put it down when her stomach began churning. "Janet insisted that all she had to do was catch the eye of the right director, the right agent, the right somebody. And then—" She broke off, fighting for control. "Some backstreet operator convinced her she needed a credit to interest the right people. If she would appear in one of his films, her star would rise."

Nick ran his fingers up into his hair and supported his head, elbows on knees. "Oh, hell. . . ."

"We pieced the story together afterward," Carla said, staring ahead. "She was too modest to strip naked with a strange man in front of a roomful of people and cameras, so they gave her pills to get her through that first porno film. And the next one, and the next. Finally she took too many pills. Just twenty-two, not even important enough for her death to make the papers."

"Oh, Lord, sweetheart."

"I wasn't there for her when she needed me most. I was too busy with my own life and some guy I thought I loved."

Nick put his arms around her rigid body. "Let it go, Carla—it's too heavy a load to carry."

His soft voice melted the control she'd maintained

for so long, and the gates opened. She held on to him for all she was worth, keening over the pain, tears flooding from her eyes. He murmured her name and his love over and over, riding out the storm, anchoring her.

Her weeping receded into sighs and hiccuping, the beat of his heart and the rise and fall of his breathing steadying her. After a few moments she became aware of Pip nosing her, looking up with worried eyes. Snaking out a hand, she rubbed his ears, giving a watery laugh that broke in the middle. "Guess I must have scared you guys silly."

Nick blew out a breath. "Damn near, but what else are we good for?"

"Lots and lots, at least you. I'm not sure about Pip."

Petting her tousled hair, he said against her ear, "I'm glad I could help you get that out of your system. I'll bet you've never cried about it before."

"I've been afraid to." Realizing her face was blotched and her eyes were swollen, she buried the ravages in the curve where his shoulder and neck met.

"I'm glad you told me. I thought you wouldn't go back because you didn't want to commit to me."

Carla popped up her head. "Oh, no, Nick, it's not you. It's the movie business you're mixed up with. That's the trap that killed Janet, and I can't forgive it . . . them. . . . I can't bring myself to go back. Not even for you." She pulled out of his arms. "I better go to the bathroom and try to pull myself together."

After dousing her face with icy water, she repaired the ravages as best she could with makeup from her purse. When she came back to the living room, Nick had put on a clean T-shirt and made fresh coffee. He was sitting on the sofa, frowning contemplatively. "The world as I've always known it has tumbled upside down," he said when she sat down.

She took a sip of sweet, rich coffee, then put the mug on the blue box. "What do you mean?"

He glanced at her and took a giant, very frightening step. "I've figured out that being in love means I want to be with you for the rest of my life. And now I'm trying to map trails through that new wilderness. I'm trying to figure out some way to stay in the valley."

A flame of hope flared, but sputtered down when Carla noticed a twitch jumping under Nick's left eye. "I don't want you to give up your entire life for me, camera bum. I fell in love with a ramblin' man, and I'd never ask you to change."

He bit into his upper lip for a moment, then sighed deeply. "I'm thirty-two years old, and I only just realized how lonely my life has always been. Now that I've found you, it's time to think of settling down. This valley seems as good a place as any."

Joy swept through Carla. She put her hands on either side of his face, kissing him on the lips and the eyes. "Are you sure, darling?"

"I'm as sure of you as I've ever been of anything," he whispered, curling his arms around her. "So, how do people occupy themselves and make a living here?"

"It's difficult, for the most part. I have no idea what there might be for a man of your peculiar talents."

"And even more peculiar disabilities."

Carla smoothed his frown with her fingertips. "I've been thinking . . . maybe I should move into the jockey house. That way we could give each other pats on the head whenever necessary, because I have a feeling we might need 'em before this is all straightened out."

He gazed blankly at her the few seconds it took for her suggestion to sink in, then a brilliant smile lit his face. "Did you say you'll move in with me?"

Her grin was just as bright. "It seems I remember you inviting me, didn't you?"

"Well, you bet!" His grin turned sassy. "But what'll
Amazing Grace say if you sacrifice your reputation
on Papa's place, right in plain sight for all the world
to see?"

"I didn't think of that! You're right; it was a scandalous idea." Jumping up, Carla made for the door.

"Hey, wait a minute, I wasn't serious!" Nick grabbed
her arm. "Where are you going?"

She glanced back, laughing. "Why, over to the
house to start packing, silly."

Nine

Carla ran upstairs to her room. On the way, she poked her head through Grace's door. "You in bed already?"

Propped on pillows, her aunt was wearing a flannel nightgown against the night chill of September, and held an open book in front of her face. "Well, I ain't standin' on my head in a hammock."

Carla sat down by her feet and picked at the yarn knots of the old-fashioned quilt, biting back the elated smile she couldn't wipe off her face.

"Uh-*huh*!" Grace murmured, eyes twinkling. "You look like you been through some kinda storm, and right after I noticed lights in the jockey house again." Her wrinkles rearranged themselves into a sweet, affectionate smile. "I take it you've gone and let yourself fall in love with that citified wildman, have you?"

Carla pulled her feet up and hugged her knees, laughing softly from the sheer joy of it. "Yes, I have, Auntie. And he loves me too."

"Well, ain't that somethin'?"

"It's somethin', all right, since we still don't have one single thing in common."

Grace marked her place in the book and set it

aside. "Who the hell cares if you got anything in common—just don't drag your feet and lose 'im." Heaving up off her pillows, she reached out and gave Carla's thigh a slap. "If you're so much in love, then why don't you go move into that jockey house with 'im?"

Carla gave a surprised laugh. "I'm scandalized you'd suggest such a thing!"

"Forget scandal! Forget everything but the two of you!" The old woman gave an impatient grunt. "Let me relate an object lesson to you. My papa was a proud man and thought the Hudsons were better than most. He didn't approve of me and Lester as a couple. While I was seesawin' back and forth, wondering where my loyalties lay, that damn fool Lester went out and got another girl pregnant. I had to wait thirty years until his wife died before I got what I shoulda took in the first place."

Carla clasped Grace's hand. "That's so sad."

"Oh, pshaw, it's water over the dam. The point is, don't make the same mistake."

"I have no intention of doing that. The only reason I'm here is to get my toothbrush and spend the night with Nick. Tomorrow I'm going to pack up my things and move in."

Grace settled back on the pillows. "Well, why didn't you say so? What're you hangin' around for—my permission?"

"No, I dropped in for advice. Do you have any idea how a man like Nick could make a living here the valley?"

"A man like Nick . . . ?" The old woman frowned. "There's not much any man can do in a western valley but run cattle, raise sheep, or grow wheat. Construction, logging, mining, outfitters." She propped a finger on her saggy chin, considering the problem from all angles. "He's been to college—maybe he could teach cameras and movies at the university up in Missoula. Right here in Hamilton there's Rocky

Mountain Labs and Ribi Immuno Research." She snapped her fingers. "He oughta be a natural for BVTV, that little old public station right down the road."

Carla's face burst into a sunshine smile of optimism. "Oh, Auntie, I had no idea there were so many possibilities." She laughed in pure joy and jumped off the bed to rush toward the door. "Gotta go grab my things and start making a home for that camera bum."

A week later, Carla was standing on a chair, threading a sunny café curtain on a rod in the kitchen of the jockey house. Nick was sitting on the floor a few feet away, antiquing the old wood dinette table with a kit. "The view from down here is fantastic," he murmured. "Is this job of mine by any chance one that could be put off until later?"

She glanced down to see his paintbrush motionless in his hand. Desire curled through her body when she realized his dark eyes were aimed up her legs and under her short shorts. "Lecher. Is that all you ever think about?"

"Damn right."

"Thank goodness," she said, laughing. "Unfortunately, no, the table can't be put off mid-job. So hurry it up, and then we can discuss those more interesting bedroom chores."

"Slave driver," he grumbled, attacking the table with a vengeance.

Carla smiled, thinking about the seven heavenly days she'd spent with Nick, laughing, loving, and talking away every hour they had together. Each experience had been a wondrously fascinating discovery, every moment precious. Her hands were still on the bright curtain when she remembered that the end still loomed, unresolved. "You said you were going out to talk with the people at BVTV today. But you didn't mention whether they were receptive."

The light, bright look on his face darkened, and he jabbed the brush at the wood, making a blot that he had to rub away. "Sure, they were happy as clams to see me."

From her position on the chair, all she could see was the top of his head. "Well, were there any opportunities for you?"

"Unfortunately, no—that's why I didn't mention it. They were delighted to see me, only because they anticipated the free use of my electronic and photographic equipment, and maybe have me contribute my experience and time—gratis. But nothing that pays a salary."

"Bummer," she said, hiding her disappointment as she eyed his frustrated, slapdash painting motions. "How about Grace's other leads?"

He glanced up at her, hiding his feelings with a cocky grin. "Well, with my little problem, I hardly think teaching at the university or working at an immunology lab is exactly me, do you?"

"For heaven's sake, Nick, both you and I know you're smart enough that your little problem wouldn't hold you back if you wanted to do something," she declared staunchly. "The real problem is that I can't picture you sitting at a desk or standing in a lecture hall for eight hours a day."

"True enough." He nodded his agreement. "And I also can't picture myself raising cows or grubbing in the soil, which takes expertise I don't have one ounce of. So much for ranching." Putting the brush down, he rubbed the stain into the creases and corners of the table, then glanced up with a grin. "But I suppose I could go out in the mountains and prospect for gold. Isn't that what you thought I was doing, first time you saw me?"

She laughed. "I expect you could starve as ably as any of the others, trying that."

"You betcha."

Carla finished hanging the curtain and stood back to admire the effect. "What do you think?"

Nick looked up and nodded. "Love them. The kitchen is beginning to look real cozy. The whole house is," he said, glancing through the archway into the living room, where she'd put bright slip-covers on his junk furniture and added real pieces from the attic of the ranch house, and placed rugs on the floor, and pictures on the walls . . . so much warmth. "I didn't realize you were a miracle worker."

"I'm not," she said, flushing with pleasure over his praise. "This is such a lost cause of a house, even a few touches of color and some doodads can work wonders."

He smiled tenderly at her. "It looks like a miracle to me, because this is the first real home I've ever had. So I sure as hell hope I can . . ." He let the sentence die, his face tightening with anxiety, and applied himself to the task at hand.

Carla sat down on the chair she'd been standing on and watched him daub at the table. "You know, I'm not exactly clear as to why you can't operate Wilderness Enterprises out of the valley."

He rubbed the last stain into the white undercoat and sat back, admiring his job. "Because what I've been doing depends upon networking, meeting the right people—things like that."

"Well, it isn't like we're cut off from the world, you know. We actually have telephones, airplanes, and even a post office."

Nick glanced up at her and smiled slightly. "Sure you do, but did you know it takes *two* days to get express mail in and out of Hamilton? And has it occurred to you that I might have reached the Amazon Indians in time to get the film if I'd been in Los Angeles?"

"No, I guess it hadn't."

He began picking up his antiquing materials, frowning heavily. "Actually, I could run the Enterprise from here, if Bunny would stay with me. I already asked her, but she said she's no small-town kind of girl, so we'd have to part company." He twisted his lips into a smile. "I might be the backbone of the Enterprise, but she's the nerve network that makes it go. I'd have to hire ten secretaries and a magician to take her place. No, without Bunny I'd be better off selling the corporation."

Carla nodded. "So what do we do next?"

"I'm going to talk with the forest service and see what goes on in the mountains around here."

On the following Saturday Preston Mann filmed a scene outside St. Mary's Mission, a tiny, steepled church built by the priests who had answered the Flathead Indians pleas for "blackrobes." There was a gathering of "settlers" and real Indians outside the church, all of them costumed. Grace, in her traveling dress, and several other local extras were mingling with the professional cast.

Carla and Nick watched from the sidelines, holding hands. She stared at the church, trying to ignore whispers and murmurs of the past drifting about on the breeze. He must have felt them, too, because he mused, "It is really weird to think that old Pierre might have helped build this church."

"Yes, and it makes everything so much more real," she said, watching as the scene of Emily and Michel's first meeting progressed, the boy with the headband and the girl with golden hair making shy eyes at each other. Pres was cursing over the unscheduled breeze that insisted upon ruffling the young couple's clothing and hair.

Everyone went silent and motionless while the cameras rolled, but after the cry of "cut!" Nick said, "I talked to the forest service yesterday."

"What did you find out?" Carla glanced eagerly at him, desperate to hear something positive.

Her optimism sagged when his expression turned grim. "Logging used to be top business around here. The lumber companies would have gladly stripped the hills bald, if the forest service hadn't closed their operations down. The environmentalists are fighting to keep them from coming back and finishing the strip. Besides logging, some characters are pushing for a mine that'll rip the entire top off a mountain in the Sapphires. Half the population of the valley actually wants it to happen. Can you believe that?"

Spirits sinking to the bottoms of her feet, Carla put her arm around his waist, feeling the need to hold him close for as long as possible. "Doesn't sound like anything you'd care to become involved in."

Nick muttered something blue under his breath, then shut up when the cameras began rolling again.

"I can't believe it's the end of October already," Gayle said, taking a break between patients to eat her lunch at Carla's salon. "The weather had been so gorgeous, but I don't suppose it can last much longer."

Bunny had dropped in to have Carla wash and blow-dry her hair. "Yeah, things are frantic on site, since the shoot has to be finished before the snow flies. Pres is beginning the final scene this afternoon, and that's the last of it. *Finis.*" She snapped her gum gleefully. "Then it's back to civilization for me, and none too soon, I say."

Carla's heart plummeted, and the blow dryer in her hand jumped. "They're doing the last scene today?! But it's not even November yet. Indian summer isn't over."

"I guess things went better than expected."

"Now, that's certainly something that depends upon your viewpoint," Carla said.

"It can't be so much of a surprise—the Enterprise's lease is up in two weeks. I thought you'd be eager to kick us Californians out as soon as possible, since you didn't want us in the first place. Except Nick, of course."

Carla ran her fingers through Bunny's mane of blonde hair, giving it a final distracted fluff. "I guess my priorities have changed over the summer."

Gayle took the last bite of her sandwich and threw her plastic bag in the basket. "Is Nick planning to go on writing screenplays, now that he's had one filmed?"

"Well . . . I don't know . . . he's never mentioned it." Carla brightened. "Maybe he *could* do that if this movie turns out to be a success."

"Hey, it's twelve—gotta go." Bunny jumped out of the chair and walked to the door. "Press is filming at two, and I don't want to miss one sob of the final breakup scene."

Carla suddenly realized that precious minutes she could be spending with Nick were flying past at an accelerated rate. "Take my appointments, Jill. I don't know when I'll be back," she said over her shoulder as she ran for the door.

Nick paced in an agony of restlessness through the deserted jockey house, Pip dogging his steps. The prospects were looking grimmer by the minute. His spirits were so low, they were dragging behind his heels.

On the one hand, he loved Carla with a force that shook him though and through. On the other, he knew his hyperactive self well enough to realize he'd go out of his mind if he didn't have a project, a challenge, a crusade, *something* to burn off his inner fervor.

He paced through the cozy little nest she'd created in the short month they'd been together. For a long time he stood in the center of the bedroom, breathing in the scent of Carla's perfumes. He gazed at the flowered comforter on the bed where they'd loved—loved frantically, it seemed to him now. Talked, touched, laughed, teased, filling every moment as if terrified it wouldn't last. He hit the wall with a fist. It would last! He'd make it happen. Somehow.

Pacing back to the living room, hands stuffed in the pockets of his tan cords, Nick gazed at the pictures on the walls, many of them photos he himself had taken. It seemed unfaithful to Carla for him to feel the siren call of the jungles, rivers, mountains, aborigines, so he was trying to purge those yearnings from his system. Frustrated, he kicked the sofa leg and, like a tiger in a cage, began another round of pacing. Coming full circle, he jumped, his body prickling with surprise.

Carla was standing in the open door, achingly beautiful in blue tights and a tunic sweater, holding a brown bag. He hadn't even heard the car drive up, but it was obvious she'd been standing there for some time, watching him agonize. "It isn't going to work, is it?" she said quietly, her voice husky with sadness.

"Yes, it is going to work," he said stubbornly. "I'll make it work."

She bit her lip to steady her quivering chin. "Now how are you going to do that, camera bum? You've been living a domestic life for only a month, and you're already going crazy being tied down here."

Nick glanced irritably around the house he'd come to love. "It isn't being tied down *here* that's making me crazy!" he exclaimed, tearing his fingers through his hair. "It's this damn valley."

She folded her arms across her midriff, stiffening herself to be very understanding and accepting. "Yes, I felt that way when I came back home too. I missed the things a big city can offer . . . plays, the symphony, freewheeling thinking. Rural life can be boring to the uninitiated."

"'Boring'! I'll never be bored as long as you're around. And I can take or leave plays and such. I'm not a sit-around kind of guy."

Her understanding was beginning to wear thin. "Then what *is* your problem?"

Frustration and anger began stewing inside Nick again. "What's my problem? My problem is that the valley isn't boring *enough*. Outside people have begun flocking in to retire, or build summer homes, snapping up the best land, bringing in smog, litter, crime. All that damn building and construction going on everywhere. They're even building camping complexes in the most beautiful wild areas, for Lord's sake."

He resumed his trapped pacing. "Doesn't anyone realize this is one of the last pure, natural areas in the country? It makes me furious to see the residents fighting anyone who wants to protect and preserve it."

Carla leaned against the door frame and listened quietly until his spiel ended. Then she said, "A lot of people in the valley barely make enough money to live on, so naturally they aren't receptive to environmentalists. Growth of any kind will help feed their children through a long, jobless winter."

Everything she said made so much sense, it infuriated him. "You, too, Benedict Arnold?" he snapped irritably.

Matching frustrated anger reddened her face. "Oh, for heaven's sake, be reasonable, Nick! The valley is suffering from chronic economic depression. And it seems to me you ought to give the people as much consideration as you do ecology."

He stared at her, knowing damn well she had as strong an ecological conscience as he did, despite her flare-up. And he couldn't figure out why in the devil he was picking a fight with her, because all he wanted was to find some impossible Shangri-la and live with her forever. Sighing, he rubbed his hands over his face. "Sorry. I guess I snapped at you because I'm in an economically depressed phase, too, after throwing every penny I ever saved into the movie. I need to start making a living pretty soon, but—"

"But what?" Carla whispered, her face going visibly pale.

He swallowed audibly around a lump in his throat. "But I can't bring myself to make a living by helping transform this beautiful valley into urban blight. I don't think I can stay here."

"I know you can't, darling," she said in a tremulous voice. "I've known it from the beginning."

It tore at his heart to see her beautiful violet eyes become glittery with tears; it felt like a poison dart piercing him, to know he was hurting her. "I wish you'd get mad and scream and cry and yell at me. I deserve it."

Carla shook her head and forced a weak little smile. "No, you don't, darling. I fell in love with a ramblin' man, and I wouldn't have you any other way."

Pip yelped when Nick tripped over him in his rush to wrap his arms around her. "Oh, sweetheart, I love you so much and I do want to settle down and be with you. I am going to; I just don't have all the snags worked out yet."

Carla wrapped her arms around his neck in a stranglehold and began to kiss him, agonized by not knowing how long they had—another week, a month? "Oh, please, make love to me, Nicky. Quickly, do it now."

"Oh, yes, sweetheart, yes, I want you so badly." With an urgency that equaled hers, he nibbled at her lips and probed her with his tongue, until she shuddered and moved against him.

Slowly, they made their way into the bedroom without separating. She stood quietly, filled with unshed tears, her breath coming in quick, uneven gasps as she watched him take off his clothes, one piece at a time until his magnificent body was bared before her. She touched him, ran her hands over his muscles, his scars, the shaft of his passion.

With trembling hands, Nick lifted the sweater over her head and off, and worshipfully cradled his hands under her breasts, his dark eyes filled with love as he gazed at her face. Slowly, in a caress, he slipped her tights and panties off together and lifted her onto the bed, then lay beside her.

They didn't speak; everything had been said. They didn't get out the packet . . . for this once, nothing would come between them. By now he knew the exact formula to bring her to shuddering, aching need. He kissed her mouth, then left a wet, burning trail of kisses down her neck, over her breasts, down her stomach. She cried out when his tongue and then his fingers probed her. "Oh, please, darling, I want more, all of you. Now."

"Yes, now, sweetheart." He raised himself and covered her, entering to lie still a moment. "I am all yours. You do know that, don't you?" he whispered, lifting his head to look down into her face.

She held him desperately and nodded. "Yes, I do, darling. I know how you love me."

Lowering his head, he covered her mouth, filling her with his tongue, teasing her and himself until desire washed their minds clean of worries and dread about the future.

Groaning, Nick took her wildly, furiously—just as she wanted him to do—until they both cried out with the agony of release. When it was over, doom had been eradicated for the time being. They lay entwined, holding each other. Smiling with contentment, Carla nestled her cheek on his shoulder and played with the hair on his chest. "So that's what a nooner is."

Resting his cheek on her tousled, chestnut hair, he gave a soft laugh. "Haven't you ever had one before?"

"No, but I suppose you have."

"I'll never tell. Come to think of it, what *are* you doing home at noon? Did Hudson's Hair self-destruct?"

"No, Jill is holding down the fort for however long, because I wanted to spend as much time as possible with you."

Nick cuddled her closer, drawing circles on her shoulder with a fingertip. "That's nice, but what brought it on?"

"Bunny told me Pres is shooting the final scene of the movie this afternoon."

"Oh, yeah, that." His deep sigh lifted his chest under her head.

"You knew? Why didn't you tell me?"

"Guess I didn't want to face it."

After the brief respite, doom had reared its head again, and Carla had to pinch her lips together to stop them from trembling. She didn't want to face it either, and pulled away from him, turning the other way. Then she quickly reached over the edge of the bed to rescue her brown bag out from under Pip's interested nose. "Anyhow, whatever, I brought a couple of packages of cupcakes for lunch—want to have a junk-food fix with me?"

He rubbed his hands over his face. "Either that, or get raving drunk."

They lay on their backs, side by side, and dined on sticky sweetness. Licking his fingertips, Nick balled the wrapper and flicked it into the valley between Carla's bare breasts. "So, here's a status report. I explored all the opportunities I can think of here in the valley, and came up with zilch." He hesitated, then asked, "So let's look at the other side of the coin. Is there any chance you might be able to forget the past and come back to California?"

Carla picked up his balled wrapper and studied it intently while she considered the possibility. She pictured Janet, remembered her going downhill, withdrawing, dead in a morgue. Still, that was three years ago. Now was now, and this was Nick. She turned her head and studied his face, loving every feature—his jutting nose, his midnight eyes that were filled with love for her. "If I should put forth the effort and make myself ignore the past and go back with you—then what?"

His brows sank thoughtfully over his eyes. "That's something I haven't blazed trails into yet. I don't know . . . make another home? Live together? Love. That sounds like paradise to me."

"It ought to, from your end. But what am I supposed to do back there in Los Angeles while you're off trekkin'?"

"I don't know. What do the women of servicemen do?"

She rolled over toward him and put her arms around his wonderful, hairy chest. "Well, most of them are . . . uh . . . wives, and they gather in groups and raise their children."

"Wives . . . ?" Nick looked so panicked, she had to laugh.

"Don't worry, I'm not planning to get out a shotgun and force you into anything, camera bum. But I will think about going back to California and living in sin with my lover—since I don't care for the alternative, which is giving you up." She swung her shapely legs out of bed. "So, let's go watch Pres shoot the last scene, okay?"

Ten

The overripe scent of dying autumn filled the valley. The aspens still had most of their leaves, liquid gold under the brilliant sun, interspersed with the dark green of the pines. Across the valley the softer Sapphire Mountains were hazy and gray-blue. In the west, the rugged Bitterroots had white caps from an early snowfall. Carla and Nick sat on the boulder where they'd sat before, on top of the ridge where he'd first told her about the movie. They watched silently as the scene was filmed.

With only a couple of hours of good light left, the fractious voices of Pres and the crews carried as the shoot progressed with the usual fits and starts and the typically frustrating breaks and fluffs.

Grace, in long skirts and a bonnet, was among a group of settlers. The Indians were on horses, their tepees and belongings packed on a travois, the French trapper and his family with them. A baby cried, a couple of dogs snarled in a spat, horses snorted; otherwise the Indians were silent in grief over leaving their beloved valley forever—five times.

In the sixth sequence the young lovers interacted as the Indians began leaving forever still another time. At the very end of the line came the boy in the headband, sitting rigidly on a pinto pony. The golden-haired girl stood at the fringes of the settler group, watching.

In bits and pieces, the tragedy unfolded. The girl ran forward, calling the boy's name. He wheeled his horse and began galloping back. Before they came together, her angry father called out and aimed his rifle at the boy. The girl ran back to grapple with him for his weapon. The trapper grabbed the pinto's rein and dragged his son away, galloping to catch up with the Indians.

The girl's long-drawn-out scream echoed through the woods and hills. Then silence. An eerie whispering cry in the pines on the ridge echoed it, as if unhealed wounds had been abraded and brought to life.

Pres had them shoot the scream a total of seven times before the light went. With each take the breeze wept anew around the trees and rocks, touching Carla's skin with a prickle of goose bumps and premonition. She imagined herself in the girl's place, screaming after Nick. Torn from him. Oh, God, how could she bear to lose him like that?

Finally the cry rose from below, "It's a wrap!"

She dashed the heels of her hands against the tears flowing down her face, and though they were mostly over her own painful confusion, she murmured, "Oh, poor, poor Emily."

"Poor, poor Michel." Nick put his arms around her shoulders, pulling her close, smiling his love. "Emily should have gone with him."

"Yes . . . I suppose," she whispered, turning to hold him tightly. "But if she had, there would have been a whole different tribe of Leclercs running around. And I would never have met you. You wouldn't even have been born."

He laughed softly against her hair. "No great loss to the world."

"It'd have been a terrible loss—especially to me."

Carla rested her cheek on his shoulder, watching the jubilation going on among the triumphant crews down below. She wondered if her love for Nick was strong enough to conquer her aversion to Movieland, USA. But what kind of a life could they lead when she felt as she did about that culture? She began to feel so confused and torn she thought she'd go insane. She didn't even fully understand why her inner instincts fought so strongly against her going back, when she so dreaded letting Nick go.

A glimmer of optimism gleamed when she remembered there were a few options they hadn't discussed yet. She lifted her head to smile at him. "You did it, darling. Your dream has come true and Pierre's tale is on film." Bending forward, she kissed him on each cheekbone, his nose, and the scarred brow, and then on the lips. "I'm so proud of you for writing such a beautiful story."

"Aw, it was nothing, just dumb luck," he said, his grin cocky and his dark eyes gleaming with pride. He matched her congratulatory kisses with victorious ones. "But it's nice having a fan club."

"Maybe the movie will make you a big success and bring you fame and fortune."

"Wouldn't that be something? Of course, everyone always hopes they've produced a sleeper," he said, still grinning. "But unfortunately, Pres's company is small potatoes, so we're just praying the film will recoup production costs before sinking out of sight without a ripple."

She sighed; so much for that option. "Well, at least you can show the film to your granddad. He'll give it five stars, I bet."

He laughed affectionately. "Right. He's the reason I wrote it, so I guess I *am* a success."

"I should hope so, because even if the movie should happen to sink, you have the script on your resumé now. That should give you a leg up in having another accepted." She ran her fingers through his tousled black hair. "Seems as if screenplays are something that can be written in a little western valley, aren't they?"

His triumphant smile faded and his brow contracted in frustration. "They could, yes—don't you think I thought of that? I've been driving myself crazy trying to come up with an idea for another plot—something, anything—but nothing develops. All I had in me was Pierre's story."

Carla sighed even deeper as her last option bombed. "Well, then, I suppose I'll have to think more seriously about going back to California. It seems as if at my advanced age, it's about time for me to grow up and rise above my aversion."

Hope and joy lit his face like a lamp. "Do you really mean it? You'll come back with me?"

She tensed apprehensively over his anticipation. "I didn't say that, darling. I said I'd think about it."

"Well, thinking about it is a step up from a flat no." Nick hugged her close and rained kisses up and down her neck, then lifted his head. "Listen, everything has been ready for weeks to hold a wrap party the day the shoot is over. These movie people you waged war against can't wait to get out of here. Why don't you come on down and look them over. They aren't such a bad lot of people, you know. Mingling might help you make a positive decision."

Carla looked at the people putting away their equipment down below. "Okay, why not?"

"Great! Wanna come as my date, Miz Scarlett?"

She felt as if her insides were frozen into a lump of anxiety, but she forced a laugh. "Well, la, Rhett, I don't believe you've ever asked me out on a date before. How can I say no?"

"Hey, did I tell you how much I love seeing you dressed as a cowgirl?" Nick said as they walked down the lane toward Little Hollywood.

The sun had slipped behind the mountains and there was a brisk late-autumn bite in the night air. Carla was wearing a fringed suede jacket along with her pointy boots and tight western pants. The jacket kept her skin warm, but did nothing for the frozen fear inside.

"I believe you have," she said, determined to face the party with courage and a good face. She looked over his brown sport jacket, white shirt, and tan cords. "You, on the other hand, are too much of a city dude for my taste. Nothing will ever beat the outfit you had on when I first met you. What'd you ever do with the buckskin shirt?"

He laughed. "It tired to rise up on its own legs and fight after I took it off, so I burned it."

She couldn't help laughing too. "You didn't! That's sacrilege."

They walked into the plaza in the center of the circled RVs. The party had been in full swing long enough for the celebrants to have tippled freely. Shrieking and laughter competed with the heart-squeezing beat of blaring music.

"Carla! Nicky!" Press cried out, rushing out of the crowd to throw his arms around them both. "It's over! It is finished. Job well done. Get yourselves something to eat. Sing, dance, drink, and make merry!" He swirled back into the crowd.

A bizarre buffet was spread over two tables: pâté, Brie, tofu wieners, Kentucky Fried Chicken, and a little of everything else in between. Her stomach churning over the sight of food, she put down her plate unfilled and glanced claustrophobically at the swirling mass of people.

Now that the pressure was over, the crews had let down their hair and costumed themselves in anything from normal, to rhinestone cowboy, to eastern affectation, to leather, chains, and fluorescent spiked hair. Two couples were doing an almost obscene dance around a crackling bonfire. A pair of men were dancing cheek to cheek, oblivious to anyone else. Someone wolf-howled at the rising full moon, setting off shrieks.

Nick put his plate down, watching Carla intensely, his dark eyes full of sympathy and support. He put an arm around her shoulders and drew her close against the warmth and strength of his body. "I know all these people, sweetie, and they're not as bad as they look. Just kickin' up their heels."

She nodded grimly. "It isn't that, Nick. My problem is that I recognize several people who knew Janet and egged her into wanting more than she could have. I have to figure out how to forgive them."

He squeezed her shoulders. "Come on, let's go mingle. The best way to beat 'em is to meet 'em head-on."

As they walked into the crowd, Nick accepted accolades and congratulations with laughter and jokes. Carla faced cries of recognition with a facade of grace and a fixed smile. With every minute that passed she felt more closed in, as if her oxygen were being cut off.

Nick bent closer. "Need a breather?" When she nodded almost imperceptibly, he backed them out of the fray to the sidelines and observed dismally, "Not going well, is it?"

"I'm trying." She clenched a fist against her chest and watched the revelry for a while. "Oh, damn, there's Ralph!" she exclaimed suddenly.

"Who's Ralph?" Nick asked, glancing around.

"Jill's husband. That bozo over there in skintight leather pants and chains around his neck. Where on *earth* did he scratch up that outfit? And who *is* that woman he's with?" Muttering under her breath, she walked over to him. "Ralph, what are *you* doing here?"

"Havin' a goo-o-d time," he sang out, fitting his hand over the hand already tattooed on his partner's nearly exposed breast. "Same as you, Carla. I know you been cuddlin' in that little old house at your place. So don't go pullin' prissy on me."

She noticed with disgust that his eyes had a funny look and that he had a tiny spoon hanging around his neck, among the chains. "Ralph, you can't compare yourself to me. I'm not married, but you are! What about Jill?"

Grabbing her arm, he dragged her out of earshot. "I don't need you climbin' on my back. This is the first time I've ever experienced *real life*. All there is for a man in this valley is grubbin' for a few bucks, and that woman says I'm a handsome guy and she'll help me break into the movies if I treat her nice."

Nick separated Ralph's hand from Carla's arm. "I'll tell you what that woman will help you do—catch some disease you'll wish you'd never heard of. Go home to your wife."

Ralph stared at them for a moment, then whipped around and walked back to his big chance.

Carla watched him. Then her stomach heaved, and she rushed into the shadows, afraid she'd vomit. "You okay?" Nick asked, putting his arms around her.

She leaned her face into his shoulder, taking deep breaths to quell the nausea. "I'm all right," she finally whispered.

"Like hell you are, and it's fairly obvious this is another option that isn't going to work." He stroked her back with a solid, warm hand.

Clutching her arms around him, she almost cried out over a chasm she could sense cracking open between them. "Oh, Nick, I want to so badly, but I can't go back, not even for you."

"I know, sweetheart. I'd never expect you to when you feel so strongly about it." He held her solidly. "Don't worry, I'll figure something else out. Give me time."

That was the problem: Time was so critically short. Carla could almost hear the seconds ticking away on

a stopwatch as people shouted and laughed all
around them, reveling in the prospect of an immi-
nent departure. The months had shrunk to weeks,
and now there were only days. She couldn't bear to
listen any longer. "I don't feel good; I've got to get
away from here."

"Good idea. I'll take you back to the jockey house."

She drew away from Nick's arms, the fissure between them broadening as she began to accept the
fact that he belonged in this world, or more precisely
to the one these people would all go back to within
days. "No, stay here and enjoy your party. I don't
mind walking back alone."

His face settled into that stubborn expression
she'd come to know and love. "Carla, there isn't a
thing I want to stay here for. I only want to be with
you." He took her hand and led her away from the
bonfire.

They were halfway down the lane when Bunny
came running after them, yelling, "Nick, wait! Why
are you always so damned hard to find?! I've been
looking all over for you. Juan Fernandez sent a cable
that your Amazon Indians have come back, and
they're asking specifically for *you*."

He stopped short and whirled around. "You're
kidding! When?"

Carla went numb inside when she saw an excitement light up his face that rivaled the glow of the
moon and bonfire.

"He sent it only hours ago." Bunny hopped from
one foot to the other, chewing her gum at close to the
speed of sound. "Pres said his pilot could jet you
straight to LAX this time. And I managed to reserve
you a quick flight out to Brazil—leaving tonight yet.
So get your behind in gear, buster! This is hot!"

Suddenly the excitement on Nick's face blinked
out. For a moment he stood very still, head down,
and then he turned and smiled at Carla. "I'm not

going, Bunny. I've got more important things to take care of right here."

A clutch of happiness grabbed her, but it disappeared as quickly as his excitement had. Her heart sank as she watched the dynamic man fade right in front of her. The cockiness left his face, his dark eyes turned heavy and shadowed.

She loved him too much to allow his sacrifice. "Don't be ridiculous, camera bum," she said, forcing brightness. "Of course you're going. If it were any other project, I'd grab you and hang on. But I know as well as you do that if you back away from this, the world will lose a record of that dying people. It's not your choice, it's your obligation to go and do this."

He hung back, searching her face, torn: wanting to go, wanting to say. "I suppose you're right."

"Of course I am—the man who would drop everything and rush after this rainbow is the man I fell in love with. So, hurry up, will you? I'll help you pack and drive you to the airport."

Life regenerated in his face. "Well . . . okay, let's go."

Pandemonium erupted. Bunny rushed to town for dehydrated survival rations that might not be available in a primitive country. Carla and Nick rushed around the jockey house, bumping into each other as they located first aid kits and jungle gear, then dumped them with his safari clothes into a suitcase. His cameras, film, and tape recorders were packed more tenderly in a solid crate.

Carla didn't have time to feel anything in that hour of frenetic activity. But her heart seemed to fly into pieces when Bunny exploded into the house. "The Learjet's fueled and the pilot's into his countdown. You gotta leave now if you want to make it to LAX in time to catch your southbound flight."

Throwing everything into Nick's sport wagon, they burned rubber, making it to the tiny airport and out onto the apron in ten minutes. Bunny hopped out, yelling at the pilot to stow everything in the plane.

Nick drew Carla into the shadow of a building, away from the few feeble airport and runway lights. Bathed in the glow of the full moon, he put his arms around her and buried his face in her hair. "I feel as if I'm being pulled apart, sweetheart. I've wanted to go and do a film of these Indians for so long. But oh Lord, I hate leaving you, especially when nothing is settled between us."

She wrapped her arms around his neck, straining to hold him closer. "Darling, it's time we both faced the truth: Ramblin' is you. I saw it in your face when Bunny gave you the message."

"Nick, come on," Bunny called from the plane.

"In a minute!" he called back, and kissed Carla's neck from her collarbone to her ear. Then he kissed her on the lips, nibbling and tugging, delving into her mouth with his tongue, sending aching tendrils of desire creeping through her body.

Lifting his head, he looked down at her, his eyes caressing the shape of her face and soul. "If all goes as I hope, I don't know how long I'll be gone. At least several weeks, possibly a few months. But I'll be back as soon as I can, sweetheart."

Carla knew what she had to do. Only because she loved him so much did she find the strength to pull free of his arms. She drew in a fractured breath. "I think it would be best if you didn't come back."

His chin jerked up as if she'd hit him. "What . . . ?"

"Nick, being with you this summer—" Her voice broke; she bit her lip and went on, "Being with you has been beautiful, but we both knew from the beginning that we'd only last until Indian summer was over. It was fun to dream of more, but . . ." She lifted her shoulders and let them drop. "Well, it's pointless to drag things out."

"You can't mean that!"

"Yes, I do." Her eyes blurred; she was hurting so

badly she felt faint, but forced herself to continue. "It makes good sense to cut off a summer affair quick and clean, so we can get on with our lives."

"How can you call what we had an 'affair'?!" The blue-white light of the moon shone cold on the pain growing in his face. "You didn't really love me at all, did you?"

A sort of paralysis stopped her from crying out in anguish; she'd never, never wanted to hurt him. "Oh, Nick, I did—*I do!* I love you with all my being. But you'll wither away if you stay here, and you know it as well as I do! We'd destroy each other."

He jumped when Bunny shouted from the plane. "Nick, come *on!*

"*In a minute!*"

"Go, Nick, please," Carla cried out desperately, clasping her hands together so she wouldn't reach out and hold him back. "The longer you stay, the harder you make it. There isn't anything more to say. All that's left is the forgetting."

The agonized torment and confusion in his eyes ignited into frustrated anger. "*Dammit!* If that's what you want, then, baby, that's what you've got. But don't you stand there so smug telling me you're going to forget me. Because you aren't. You're going to lie awake the rest of your life remembering how we—"

Breaking off, Nick jerked her into his arms, forcing her back against the building. He bruised her lips with his kiss. Going weak with the delicious force of him, Carla breathed his essence, greedily storing his taste, his scent. She memorized his body as the hard muscles of his arms crushed her against him, flattening her breasts against his chest. His thighs and the curve of his pelvis thrust against her, sapping her strength.

Suddenly he gave a convulsive sob and released her as suddenly as he'd grabbed her. Huddling against the building, she bit her teeth together against calling him back as he ran toward the plane. He leaped up the steps, paused at the door, half-turned, threw back his head, and let out a roar of grief, then ducked inside without looking back.

Carla felt as if her heart was ripping apart as the jet swept down the runway and shot up toward the glittering nigh sky. In seconds the blinking red and green lights disappeared. In a minute the noise faded into the distance.

"Good-bye, Nicky," she whispered from a great vacuum of silence and despair.

Eleven

Pip yelped his welcome when Carla climbed out of the car. He tried to lead her to the moonlight-bathed jockey house, thinking that's where she belonged. "Nick is gone, Pip," she said, gazing across the ranch yard at that symbol of the happiness she'd sent away. "And I hurt him so badly, he'll never trust me enough to come back."

Peaked ears drooping, he whined as if he comprehended more than the sadness in her tone. For once he didn't try to bull his way into the ranch kitchen when she opened the door, but just sat on the stoop, staring mournfully across the yard. "Oh, you dumb dog, get in the house and quit looking like that!"

Together they plodded down the hall toward the stairs, tiptoeing past the den, where Grace and Lester were watching TV. Carla couldn't face them quite yet. Climbing the creaky old stairs on feet of lead, she walked into her room. Once, when her childhood had fallen apart, she'd found comfort there. But now, sitting numbly on the bed, the heeler's chin resting on her knee, she began to realize that nothing, *nothing*, could ease her pain this time.

A moment later Grace poked her head through the

door, her faded eyes anxious and questioning. "I thought I heard you sneak in. Somethin' wrong?" She took in the expression on her niece's face. "Nick's gone and left, ain't he?" she said softly.

Carla swallowed around the lump of tears caught in her throat and nodded.

The old woman puffed up like a bantam rooster. "Did that bastard break it off?!"

"No, I was the one who sent him away. It would have destroyed him if I'd let him stay."

Hobbling into the room, her aunt sat down on the bed, opening her arms as she had so many years before. Once again Carla went into them and wept in misery on Grace's shoulder. Anguished, bitter tears poured out of her soul. There was no bottom to her grief, but eventually the weeping slowed, and finally it stopped.

"Mighta been the best thing to give 'im up—I wouldn't know about that," the old woman said, holding her close. "But I can see it hurts like hell."

Carla nodded, pulling out of Grace's arms to wipe her face on a handful of tissues. "I think I'm going to die."

"Oh, you won't die, dear—take it from the voice of experience. You'll suffer for a while, then you'll stow the pain away in the back of your mind and get on with some kinda life."

For the first time, Carla began to understand her aunt. "Did you really feel like this when you lost Lester to that other woman?"

"Half my brain cells may have rotted away with age, but the memory of that hurt is still sharp as glass." Grace smiled wryly. "Consider yourself lucky you don't have to watch your man take another wife and raise a family in front of you."

"Oh, God, I couldn't bear it." Carla took a shuddering breath. "It's not fair! First Emily lost Michel and felt this way, then you lost Lester, and now me. Is there some kind of a curse on Hudson women?"

"I don't know about a curse, but we do seem to have a talent for pickin' ourselves the most impossible man out of the lot."

"Isn't that the truth?" Carla blew her nose in sodden tissues. "I wish I could curl up and sink into oblivion. How can I go back to work and face the community feeling this way? How did you?"

Grace brushed a gnarled hand down Carla's cheek. "You go out and lift that little old pointy Hudson chin high, girl. Pretend you're above it all."

Within a week Little Hollywood was deserted. They'd cleaned up the grounds, taken the fences down, and restored everything so fastidiously that from a distance it looked as if they'd never been there.

Last of all, Bunny helped Carla pack Nick's things in boxes. "For what it's worth," she said, snapping her gum, "I know Nick loved you so much, he would have thrown away everything he treasured and stayed if you'd said the word. I also know that he would have begun to feel he had a leash and collar around his neck. You did an unselfish, brave thing in letting him go."

"I don't feel very brave."

"Tell me about it—heroines don't necessarily feel heroic."

Carla frowned, glancing at the lion-maned woman. "You said not, but you did love him, didn't you? And you set him free too."

"Did love him . . . and still do. And worse, he set *me* free."

"Does the pain ever get any better?"

Bunny blew a bubble and pulled it back in with an agile tongue. "Better get yourself a computer, honey."

After bunny drove away with Nick's things in his sport wagon, Carla walked slowly through the jockey house, bidding farewell to the little home she'd shared with him for too short a time. Her footsteps echoed in loneliness. Throwing herself on the bed where they'd made love, she spent hours soaking the pillows with tears.

Later, she closed up the house intact, hoping she could begin to forget. But little unexpected things tormented her: the scent of him on her jacket, a sales slip in a pocket for something they'd bought together. Every restaurant she entered held a memory of a meal with him. Big things were left behind too—Spook, the buckskin gelding, was growing fat and lazy in the pasture.

Her salon was haunted by the wildman who'd walked into her life. She tried to hold her Hudson chin high, but it was a strain to act normally. It was a relief, perhaps her salvation, to be able to let down her pretense when the girls got together with her after work each day, offering their shoulders for support. It was also a modicum of comfort to know Jill understood how she felt. The little stylist was almost as miserable as she after Ralph had tagged along westward with his fancy girl, his eyes on the bright lights.

One evening Bonnie was sitting in a styling chair, watching Carla sweep up. Suddenly Carla stopped and stood motionless. "Your mouth is dragging around your ankles," Bonnie said. "It's been a month—isn't it getting any easier?"

Carla stared down at a snippet of black hair she'd unearthed from under a stand; unmistakably Nick's, it had clung to her finger like a living thing when she'd picked it up. "No, it isn't getting better. Being in love is like an addiction, I guess. I can resist indulging only because I don't have access to the substance. But I'll never lose the craving."

When Jill began sniffling, she silently cursed herself for tossing out such a hurtful analogy. "Sorry, honey."

"It's not your fault," Jill said, slumped in her own styling chair. "Anyway, Ralph phoned last night to say living in California wasn't going the way he hoped. He wants me to send him money so he can come back home."

Bonnie crossed her knees irritably. "You wouldn't be dumb enough to send it to him, would you?"

"I don't know. Maybe he wasn't the best husband in the world, but it's awful lonely living by myself."

Remembering her last experience with Ralph, Carla thought Jill might be better off lonely. "Let him find a job and earn his own way if he wants to come back," she said, leaning on the broom. "He'd benefit from contemplating the consequences of his actions."

"Huh?"

"She said let the SOB stew in his own juices."

"Oh. I'll have to, because when he left, he cleaned our joint account out. One of my checks bounced before I realized. I don't have it to send, even if I wanted to."

Gayle was perched on the edge of the desk, her long legs stretched out. "You know, thinking back, I wish I hadn't been so flip about offering my shoulder for weeping when all this first started. Looks like I jinxed the whole beauty shop." She glanced at Carla. "Have you heard anything at all from Nick?"

"No, but I didn't expect to. He's been hurt before, so it was almost impossible for him to open up and trust me in the first place. He's not likely to put himself in a position where I could hurt him again." Carla toyed with his black hair between her fingers. "Besides, he's in a jungle somewhere around the Amazon, cut off from civilization for I don't know how long." A horrifying thought occurred to her. "The Indians he's filming are dangerous. I might never hear if he gets hurt or even killed down there."

Opening her drawer, she tenderly wrapped the black tress in tissue, along with the petrified white rose. Then she began sweeping again, trying to brush her anxieties and loneliness away.

• • •

Frail old Grace was a pillar of strength, and listened patiently without offering an opinion when Carla asked over and over, "Did I do the right thing?"

Only after several weeks had gone by did she crinkle her forehead and hazard to ask, "Is there any reason you couldn't have gone with him on his rambles?"

She jerked her head up, staring at her aunt. "I . . . it never occurred to me." She thought for a moment, then ambivalently shook her head. "You know how unsettled my childhood was. Well . . . I don't know . . . a stable home has always seemed so important to me."

"How about the flip side? You could sit in your stable home and let Nick spend time with you between his trips. Nothin' says a man has to be with you seven days a week all year long. Part-time must be better than zip."

Regret tormented Carla when she realized her aunt was right. "Good old hindsight—I know it now, but it didn't occur to me then. I guess Nick and I didn't get around to exploring all the options. Yes, I'd give anything to have him for just a few weeks, or even a few days out of every year—but now it's too late."

"I knew I shouldn't have opened my yap and butted in. There's no sense hashin' over mighta-beens."

Carla shook her head. "No, there sure isn't. But part-time probably wouldn't have worked anyway. Because he'd be living on the West Coast, and I still wouldn't have gone back there." She felt she had to justify her decision somehow. "What if Nick and I had children? I'd never want to bring them up in such a permissive environment."

"You grew up there and turned out pretty good."

Carla waved the observation off. "Yes, but look

what happened to Janet. And to Ralph. Sure, he acted like a hound, leaving her like that, but I feel sorry for him too. He got snared into an awfully tempting trap."

Grace snorted. "Horse pucky! ralph grew up down the road, so I happen to know he's been a lazy carouser all his life. It's nothin' new for him to dabble in things and get high. He's been gettin' drunk with the boys and goin' home to rough Jill up ever since they've been married."

"He roughed her up?" Carla stared at Grace, horrified. "But she never told me!"

"There's lots of little secrets hidden away in this valley you think is such a paradise. That sorta thing happens too often when life is tough." Grace peered at Carla and chanced bringing up a sensitive subject. "If you weren't so blinded by your false guilt over Janet's death, you'd see California is as good a place as any other."

"But it's not false guilt. I could have stopped Janet if only I had—" She broke off, thinking clearly for the first time in over three years. If only she'd what? Put the girl in shackles?

The old woman nodded slowly. "I loved Janet dearly, don't get me wrong. But she was so pretty and had such winnin' ways that everyone spoiled her rotten. Face it, she used people like dishrags, includin' you, and includin' those movie folk you blame so bitterly. She expected everything on a silver platter and would have got into that mess despite what you think you should have done."

"Are you trying to tell me I ran back here to hide from a fake bogeyman?" Carla's feelings were twisted into a tangle; she pulled one strand out and nodded slowly. "I came back to the ranch because it's the only place I remembered being happy as a child, and I thought I could find that again. It was a complete flight from reality." She pinched her eyes shut. "That means I sent Nick away for no good reason."

Her aunt gazed at her sympathetically, then threw out a challenge. "So what're you gonna do about it?"

"It's too *late* to do anything about it!"

There wasn't much snow on the ground yet in mid-December. So on Sunday Carla bestirred herself to go out into the ranch yard, knowing Molly and Spook badly needed exercise. She kicked the black mare into a gallop, leading the buckskin on a rope, with Pip loping along behind.

She stopped on the ridge where an eternity ago she had first sat with Nick, looking out over a spring vista. It was brown and dead now, the river bleak, the mountains snowcapped, the sky overcast. Giving a shudder, she turned the horses, drawn as before toward the northwest.

To her surprise, a trail had been cleared to the pine grove. After tethering the horses, she walked toward the little cabin, welcomed by whispers in the boughs. To her growing amazement, she saw that the chimney, roof, and door had been restored, cleverly weathered to look as ancient as the log walls.

Inside, the debris had been removed, the dirt floor leveled and smoothed. Logs had been laid in the fireplace and a vase of flowers, dry and brown now, had been set on the mantelpiece. Her heart overflowed with tears when she realized Nick had fixed up the cabin in secret: his monument to their first lovemaking. She'd sent him away before he'd had a chance to surprise her with it.

She stumbled outside again, her mouth held open wide with mute pain, and dropped down on the log where they had teased and loved. Shivering uncontrollably with anguish, she wrapped her arms around her body and stared wildly up into the whispering boughs. "Oh, Emily, I made such a terrible mistake," she cried, her voice echoing loudly in the silence. "I wish I had followed Nick. I should never have sent him away. He's my life, my only happiness, and, oh, how I wish I could have one more chance!"

Time passed—how long she had no idea—and gradually her spirit quieted. Sympathy seemed to curl warmly around her, the boughs murmuring, *Trust, trust.* . . . She fantasized that Emily was befriending her by sharing a grief no one else could understand.

Of course she didn't believe traces of long-ago people were there; it was more likely that loneliness had driven her insane. Still, she felt so comforted that the cabin drew her back again and again over the months that followed. Each time she came away with an odd sense of optimism, as if something were in the works.

And each time she told herself that it was just more irrational, wishful thinking.

In late February, Carla came home from work windblown and half-frozen. She took off her down jacket an fur-lined boots inside the door and bee lined to the coffeepot to thaw out her gullet with a sip and warm her hands around the cup.

Grace was stirring a stew on the stove, a peculiar expression puckering her wrinkled face. Glancing first at Lester for moral support, she lifted her chin at her niece and announced, "I up and did it. I sold the damn ranch."

Carla's coffee hopped right out of the cup, splattering on the floor. For the first time in four months she'd heard something startling and upsetting enough to blow Nick out of her mind. "You did *what?*"

"Signed, sealed, and delivered the papers today. Deeded it over to the new owners." Grace dished stew into bowls, placing one at each of the three places. She studied Carla defensively, then placed her hand on the old man's shoulder, again seeking support. "I put it up for sale about a month ago, and then I got this offer and took it. Made a good deal, didn't I, Lester?" He nodded encouragingly.

Carla felt her way to a chair and collapsed, her mouth opening and closing before she could croak, "You put it up for sale? *Why?!*"

"Because the place has been nothin' but a millstone around my neck ever since Papa died. It's too much worry and work, even with your and Lester's help. I'm too old and stiff to run it."

"A millstone? But I thought you were so attached to the ranch."

"Stuck with it, not attached to it. Big difference there."

Carla stared with disbelief at her aunt, wondering if *anything* she'd ever believed was true. If Grace had never loved the ranch, she had a perfect right to sell. Logically, Carla accepted that. Illogically she was crying out inside, *But I love the ranch—what about me?* Every facet of her life was disintegrating and falling around her feet in rubble.

She picked up her fork, fingers twitching, then threw it down again. Life and feeling had begun rumbling around inside her for the first time in too long. "Why on *earth* did you do something so consequential without so much as consulting me?" she sputtered, anger bubbling up out of her frozen core. "How do you know you got a good deal? What if this new owner rooked you? I can't believe you frolicked right out and jumped willy-nilly into another major deal! Look what happened last time you did that!"

Grace glanced at Lester and blew out a breath as if she were relieved, then spooned up a bite of stew, pinky extended. "Paid some major bills last time I frolicked into a major deal, as I recollect."

Carla's face turned red with reemerging emotions. "You ruined my life, that's what you did!"

"Then if it's already ruined, this new deal can't do much more harm." Grace's faded blue eyes twinkled happily over the first spat the two had had since Nick left. "Don't worry, I learned my lesson last time, and this time I got a lawyer to do my talkin'. The deal was on the up-and-up. Sold the ranch to some young man, an agent who says he intends to develop an outfittin' business for the absent owners. He made me an offer I couldn't refuse. Never dreamt I'd get so much for the place."

Carla drummed her fingers on the table, scowling. "But what are you and Lester going to do, Grace? Where will you live? You aren't going to move into that retirement complex in Hamilton, are you? You'd hate it."

"Land's sake, no!" her aunt exclaimed, dipping homemade bread into gravy. "This time I toughed out the opposition without your help—got some rights written in the contract. You and me and Lester can stay and live in the ranch house for life."

Carla tried to imagine that grim picture in her mind. "Maybe that's all right for you, but I'll be damned if I'm going to live like a squatter on our own land."

"What you gonna do then?"

She looked from Grace to Lester, a decision roiling around inside her like a volcano about to erupt. When it blew, she smacked the table with a hand, startling Pip into a fit of yelping. "Be quiet, you dumb dog!" she snapped. "I am sick and tired of moping around this valley. I'm bored to death! I loved doing hair for stars and movies, so I'm going back to California and pick up my life. Maybe I can even track Nick down and talk him into taking me back."

Grace heaved a sigh, looking as pleased as if a seed she'd planted had sprouted. "I'll miss you like hell, dear. How soon can you go?"

"I'd like to go tomorrow—tonight!" Carla cried, fired up with anticipation over the prospect. Then reality struck. "But I have to wind up my affairs first. I can't throw poor Jill and the other stylists out on the street before they find different jobs. And if I want to start over, I need the money I've got tied up in the salon. I have to pay a loan off too. I'll leave as soon as all that's taken care of."

At the end of winter Carla was still living on the ranch and working in Hamilton. At least the snow had melted, so could visit the cabin again. Every time she went, she sensed stronger vibrations of excitement, as if a plot were rapidly coming to fruition. Which seemed ridiculous, since no one seemed eager to buy her business.

With the spring thaw, the agent for the new owner hired a crew of local men to repair and paint the ranch house and outbuildings. Carla was relieved to see they'd left the arch with Hudson and the pierced *H* brand over the driveway. It would have broken her heart to see the family name canceled out after a hundred-year occupation.

But from that point, everything went downhill.

"What in the heck is going on at your place?" Gayle asked when the girls met in Hudson's Hair the first Thursday in April. "Looks like a beehive whenever I drive past."

Carla was folding clean towels. The question goosed her temper, which was already sizzling. "'Beehive,' my foot! I call it urban blight! The lane has turned into a blacktopped road. Water and electric lines and a septic tank have been put in at the old site of Little Hollywood. Monster machines are digging basements and pouring cement foundations. There are enough carpenters swarming around to rebuild the Pentagon. They're driving me insane with their awful racket, framing up not one, but five little buildings!"

"What on earth does an outfitter need with all that?"

"He shouldn't, so mark my words: Something funny is going on." She snapped a towel straight with the sound of a rifleshot.

"Whatever, it isn't all bad. They've created jobs,"

Bonnie said. "You have an economic boom going on at your ranch."

"That same booming economy is blighting the natural beauty of the valley, at least on our ranch. I can imagine what Nick would say if he could see what's happening. After all, he has some interest in the place too."

The towel went limp in Carla's hands while she toyed with the possibility that Nick might come back and do something about the development. Then she shook her head and sighed. More wishful thinking. She'd hurt him so badly, he'd surely written her off his list.

"If it's too big an operation for an outfitter," Gayle asked, "what do you think the new owner has up his sleeve?"

"I haven't the faintest. Maybe he's going to put in condominiums, or subdivide the mountains into vacation homes. For all I know he intends to build a dump to bury nuclear waste." She snapped another towel straight. "Dammit, I wish I could get out of here and leave everything behind. Why won't anyone buy out my salon, Bonnie? I need the money I've got tied up here to start a new life."

"Takes time. The boom at your ranch hasn't reached the beauty business yet."

"Speakin' of a new life," Jill interjected, "Ralph called again last night and asked if I'd send money so he could come home."

"What'd you tell 'im?"

"Well, you know? He had me convinced I was too dumb to make it on my own, but I been doin' fine since he left. So I decided I don't need his kind of hassle any longer, and told him to go rot." She glanced at the others with a half-frightened, half-triumphant smile. "I'm gonna file for divorce."

"Oh, honey, that's wonderful!" Carla gave her a hug. "I'm glad someone around here is straightening out her life."

• • •

By mid-May, Carla was even more desperate to leave. It was heartbreaking to watch spring drift toward early summer, knowing she'd soon have to face the first anniversary of that evening when a charming, handsome, unique wildman had walked into her salon.

It rankled to know that though no one was interested in buying her salon, business was booming on the ranch. The buildings were finished and white rail fences enclosed the herds of pack mules and riding horses swarming in the pastures.

Six rather more exotic creatures turned up one day, stunning Carla to a point where she didn't notice that Pip wasn't yelping and hopping around her legs when she came home from work. "*Llamas?*" she exclaimed, walking into the kitchen. "Is the new owner turning our ranch into a zoo?"

Grace chuckled. "Ain't they darlin'? But they tend to spit atcha if you get too close."

"Really. Well, I might spit, too, because I noticed the field on the other side of the pasture is all torn up."

"It's gonna be a helipad."

"A *what?*"

"A place to land helicopters."

"I *know* that!" Carla snapped, seething over the high-tech intrusion on her precious ranch. "I'll bet you a million bucks the owner intends to parcel out the mountain end of the ranch for subdivision. He'll use the helicopter to fly buyers in and out." A thought made her go cold. "Oh, my Lord, what's going to happen to Pierre's cabin?! Someone's got to do something!"

"Like what?"

"I don't know," she cried, desperately needing someone with enough clout to help her. Her pulse leaped as she pictured the only person she knew who might join a crusade to save her own private section of the environment: Nick—if he had come out of the jungle alive! Oh, please God, let him have made it. But how could she get in touch with him? "Bunny!" she whispered, and dashed upstairs.

Spurred by excitement and myriad other emotions, Carla began searching for the phone number Bunny Fletcher had left with her. She was muttering under her breath as she scoured her room, upending boxes. But Bunny had disappeared. "Silly me!" she exclaimed, snapping her fingers. The LA operator could give her the phone number for Wilderness Enterprises. Her heart jump-started and set off racing over the thought of making the call.

She stared blindly out the window, wondering. . . . Would Nick be there, or off on another rovin' project? If he was there, would he talk to her? If he agreed to talk to her, could they work out their problems? Would they ever love again? Well, she thought, the only way to get answers was to make the phone call.

Shaking herself back into the present, she suddenly became aware of what she had been looking at through the window. The door of the jockey house was open! Her hackles rose as she realized that someone was trespassing on her most precious, personal shrine!

Racing out of her room, Carla leaped down the stairs three at a time. "New owners be damned!" she shouted to Grace as she shot out the back door. "This is war!"

Twelve

Carla stomped down the path, too incensed to realize that the very air was holding its breath in anticipation. She didn't so much as question why the black mare and the buckskin were saddled and drowsing in the corral. Striding up onto the porch of the jockey house, she stormed through the open front door.

The living room smelled musty after five months, but everything was as it had been the last time she'd walked out. Pip was stretched out on the slipcovered sofa. "How *could* you lie right there and let strangers come in here?" she hissed. He thumped his tail apologetically, but didn't move.

There were boxes of groceries and a used water glass by the sink in the kitchen. Obviously someone was moving in and wasting no time in feeling right at home. Outrage building, Carla marched down the hall. She found him in the bedroom: a tall man, muscular, in stocking feet, buttoning a white shirt from the bottom up over a magnificent chestful of black hair. Her body went so weak, she had to grab the door frame or fall. *"Nick?"*

When he jerked up his head, she saw that his face was etched with pain, his eyes dark pits under his brows and the scar a white slash in his South

American tan. He looked so thin and drawn, she wanted to cry. There was another change, too, something so intangible she couldn't grasp what it might be.

For a few beats they just stared at each other. Then he took three strides forward and grabbed her in his arms, moaning low in his throat. "Sweetheart, Carla, I—"

His voice broke and he crushed her so tightly against his body, she could scarcely breathe. Wrapping her arms around his neck just as tightly, she buried her face in his beloved scent, his texture. She soaked in the pulse and life of him, feeling complete for the first time since the night he'd left.

After a bit, Nick loosened his arms enough to look down at her, his gaze moving hungrily over her pixy features, her graceful neck, her boyish hair. Then he stepped away, his features setting themselves in stubborn, determined lines. "I'm back," he said quietly. "And we have a hell of a lot to talk about."

She nodded mutely. Oh, yes, she had so much to tell him, but when she opened her mouth to speak, all that came out was an inane, "You let someone else cut your hair. It looks awful."

His face softened as he ran his hand through black hair that fell in ragged waves over his ears and neck. "Oh, that, well, I hacked it myself while I was in the jungle."

"You've been with the Indians all this time?"

He nodded. "Until a few weeks ago. I stopped in LA to edit all the footage and put together the documentary."

"You got them on film, then?"

"Yes, and barely in time. I also ran for my life with them when the forest burned, and cried when two of their young girls were stolen by men from a new settlement encroaching on their territory. You were right: It was a project I couldn't drop, even though—" His voice broke.

She met his unwavering eyes, her insights tumbling about, begging to be revealed. "Nick, I know—"

"No, you *don't* know!" he broke in, fierce brows plunging down. "When I left last fall you said too damn much about what you *thought* you knew. You took me my surprise and didn't give me a chance to put in my two cents. Not it's my turn to talk, and I've had five, long, empty months to figure out what I'm going to say."

Carla's heart froze when she realized the hurts of the past wouldn't simply pass so easily. They had to be faced, and the end was still up in the air. She swallowed fearfully. "What did you decide to tell me?"

Nick glanced restlessly around the room. His gaze lit on the beckoning bed, then swept hungrily down over Carla's shapely body for an agonized second. "I can't talk in here," he muttered, bending over to hop on one foot, then the other, as he yanked on his boots. "I've been living outdoors in the jungle too long. I can't stand being cooped up in the house."

Her eyes had followed his to the bed, and now she tore them away and glanced at his dark, defensive face. "Why did you come back, Nick?" she asked, afraid of the answer. "It's an odd coincidence, when I was just trying to call you."

He glanced up, his expression leery of trust or hope. "Why were you?"

Just as cautious about risking her feelings, Carla went for the surface issue. "Surely you saw the changes around here when you arrived. Grace sold the ranch without so much as consulting me, and I couldn't think of anyone else but you who might help me stop the rampant development."

"Oh . . . that." Nick glanced away as if disappointed, then rubbed the back of his neck. "No, I won't help you stop it."

His answer struck her like a blow; was he *that* angry with her? "Why . . . ?"

But he was as elusive in his explanations now as the first time he'd come to the ranch. Instead of answering, he glanced at the outfit she'd worked in all day—snug-fitting white pants and a lavender shirt that played up her violet eyes. "Can you ride in those things?"

"Ride?"

A sparkle of humor lit his black eyes for the first time. "On horses—remember them? I saddled Spook and Molly as soon as I got here. I've been waiting for you to come home ever since. Are those clothes okay for riding?"

Carla glanced down at herself. "Sure, I guess."

"Good, come on then. The thing or two I have to say can be told better outside."

"Nick, I've got so much to tell you too. Everything is different now. I'm going to—"

He broke in, anxiety flaring in his eyes. "Shhh, I have to tell you my side first before you do anything!" Taking her arm, he propelled her through the little house, adding a delighted Pip to the entourage on the way through the living room.

The world outside seemed more vividly alive to Carla than it had before she'd entered the jockey house. A hymn of joy was trilling in the breeze. A riot of tulips were blooming in the yard, and the huge cottonwoods had exploded into green. Hundreds of Canada geese were flying about in a courting frenzy, silhouetted against the blaze of early-evening gold behind the western mountains.

Swinging up on Molly, Carla reined the mare a safe distance away and watched Nick hoist himself gingerly onto Spook. "Settle down, you," he bellowed when the buckskin rounded his back and bounced in circles on pogo-stick legs, exciting Pip into a rampage of yelping and whirling.

When everyone was standing on solid ground again, Carla shook her head, laughing. "Things haven't been the same since you left."

"Well, nothing was the same where I was either," he said, with not a glimmer of answering laugh, and wheeled Spook around to canter down the lane.

She kept pace, sensing again the intangible difference, the change in him. It seemed to grow stronger by the moment as they rode toward the mountains.

When they reached the ridge, Nick sent the buckskin rattling up the steep, gravelly slope, Carla following. The breeze sang an excited welcome when they pulled up the horses at the top. Looking down at the scattered cottages built on the old Indian village site, Carla was surprised to see that from up here, they resembled chalets, nature-colored to blend into the natural environment. But that didn't justify the backhoe and bulldozer, which were now lying idle in the field being torn up for a helipad.

Glancing at Nick, she tensed in reaction to his expression, a mix of pride, smugness, and anxiety. A bothersome question began rankling at her. How hurt *had* he been when she'd sent him away? "I think you'd better tell me what you know about this," she said quietly.

Raking his fingers through his ragged hair, he glanced at her evasively, then lifted the brow with the scar. "Well . . . maybe I should start at the very beginning. Let me first say that Michel and Emily's film turned out pretty well after it was edited and polished. Very authentic, subdued drama, with good dialogue, if I do say so myself. Much of it in Salish with subtitles. It'll hit the theaters next month, and the industry is already projecting it'll become a cult film, and maybe even a classic. Plowing all my money into Pres's shoestring production seems to have turned into a blue-chip investment."

Carla nodded, impatient with the change of topic. "That's wonderful, Nick, I'm really pleased for you, but about the ranch—"

He cut her off by raising his hand. "I was out of circulation in the jungle, so the news that we were going big-time sifted fairly slowly down to me. But by mid-December, when I heard, I knew what I wanted to do, so I sent a cable to Bunny to hire me a new business manager and—" He eyed Carla defensively. "I had him offer Grace a price she couldn't refuse for the ranch."

She goggled at him. "*You* bought the ranch?"

"Lock, stock, and applecart."

She stared at the complex down below, the implications of his announcement sifting slowly into the jungle of her mind. When they did, she turned toward him, her violet eyes flaring with anger. "You bought the ranch months ago? And let me suffer here, not knowing if you were alive or dead, or whether I'd ever see you again? How could you do something so sneaky and cruel, Nick?"

His tanned face reddened with matching anger. "How was I supposed to know you were suffering? You told me to get lost, as I recall!"

When it seemed they were heading for an argument, the breeze whipped impatiently around them, goosing Spook into a dance that claimed Nick's attention.

Carla watched him from Molly's back. "I thought you were such a rabid environmentalist, Nick. Whatever possessed you to turn this beautiful ranch into a . . ." She glanced at the future helipad. "Into an industrial park?!"

"It doesn't look like an industrial park, and you know it," he protested. "I had an architect design the complex so that it'll blend harmoniously with the landscape when it's finished."

"Well . . ." She had to back off from that direction, since the setting sun had gilded the complex into a veritable fairy encampment. "I still don't know how you or anyone can justify coming in and ripping up my beautiful ranch. My *home.*"

He crossed his arms over his chest, the reins dangling from his fingers. "Just remember, it's also *my* ranch and *my* home now. And who had a better right to buy it than a Leclerc?"

She cupped her hand around her mouth, trying to fight back a suspicion. He'd taken possession of the very thing she loved most; now he could do anything he wanted with it. And make her as miserable as he pleased. "Did you do this to punish me, Nick?" she had to ask.

"Punish you! Where'd you get such a bizarre idea?"

"Well . . . you were awfully angry when you left."

He balled his hands into fists. "What did you expect? Sure, I was mad as hell when you said you didn't want me back. I wasn't ready to face the truth."

The truth? A spear pierced her heart. "Nick, those things I said weren't the truth. Since then I—"

"Yes, they were the truth." His dimpled chin jerked up. "It took me a full month in the jungle, heartsick and lonely like I have never been before, to figure out you did the best thing for both of us. You were right—we couldn't have made a life together."

She cried out internally; he sounded as if there wasn't a shred of hope. "Nick, we can, I—"

"No, let me finish, now that I've started." He smiled at her for a moment, then gazed out over the valley, at the river and mountains ruddied by the sunset, at the forests, and then at the little nest of buildings below. "I also figured out a way to build myself a life in this valley."

Carla saw the gleam of pride and ownership in his eyes, and suddenly realized what had changed about Nick. The lonely quality she'd sensed from the first had disappeared. It was as if owning the ranch had given him a place in his own family history. "What life did you decide to build?"

"Over there, a few miles from here, is one of the last remaining wilderness areas of the country, with logging, mining, and uncontrolled growth nudging at its borders. So I figured the environmentalists already fighting to protect it could use a camera bum to drum up favorable publicity."

"A camera bum," she murmured, pulling Molly up when she batted her head at a too-friendly Spook.

"You betcha—this one." A touch of the old cockiness lit his grin as he jabbed a thumb at his chest. "My plan is to take influential people into the wilderness by helicopter, and then on controlled treks. After they see nature as it's meant to be, maybe a few of them will use their influence to ensure its continued preservation."

He frowned, staring at the chalets. "In the jungle I figured out that a man has to give a little to live in the real world. And that's how I justified building that little complex down there. You insisted people are as important as the environment, and you're right. I'll do my bit for the economy by keeping a crew of local people on my payroll." He blew out a breath and glanced at her. "Does that explain the chalets to your satisfaction?"

Carla nodded, a tender smile twitching her lips, then glanced toward six graceful beasts in a far pasture. "But how do you explain the llamas?"

"Oh, they make excellent pack animals." He gave a sheepish shrug. "Okay, it was a whim—I got 'em because they're cute."

"I love your little whimsies," she murmured, smiling, before turning sober again. "And I'm terribly impressed with your big ones. I withdraw my opposition, now that I understand why you bought the ranch."

"You don't understand one damn thing yet!" Spook carefully picked his way around Pip, a sleeping gray rug on the ground, when Nick reined closer and took Carla's hand. "The main reason I bought this particular ranch, sweetheart, was so that you'd be stuck with me every day, year in and year out, until I wear you down."

"Wear me down?" Carla threaded her fingers between his, locking him to her as rays of sunshine burst out of her heart.

"Yes. I quickly figured out, as I sat in that rotten jungle, that my rovin' life wasn't worth an ice cube in hell without you."

"And I was so sure you'd never come back again."

"Why'd you think that?" He slapped Spook's shoulder, raising a cloud of dust. "I practically told you flat out I would, when I left my best buddy with you."

A smug, laughing whisper in the boughs reminded her of the murmur she'd heard at the cabin . . . *Trust, trust.* She laughed, too, in amazement. "It didn't occur to me, but it should have. Someone tried hard enough to tell me."

He searched her face, probing her soul. "You did want me to come back, then?"

She gazed at him with haunted violet eyes. "Nick, I died inside after you left. It was too late when I realized I should have gone to the jungle with you, instead of sending you away."

Edging Spook still closer, he put his arms around her, a furnace of love beginning to glow in his midnight eyes. "Would you really have done something like that?"

"Well, I told you I'm a tomboy at heart." She curled her arms around his neck. "Nick, you don't plan to give up your wandering life entirely, do you?"

He frowned thoughtfully for a moment. "For some reason the obsession seemed to disappear when I bought the ranch, but . . ." He peered at her anxiously. "Well, I've been at it so long, I might be tempted to disappear into another jungle or wilderness occasionally, if an interesting opportunity happens to arise. Would that bother you?"

"No, I'm glad. You wouldn't be you if you didn't," she said, gazing at his dynamic face. "And I'll be ready to follow you to the ends of the earth."

His eyes softened with awe. "You truly do love me that much?"

She kissed his nose, his dimpled chin, the scar in his brow. "I truly do, and a zillion times more."

"Carla, sweetheart, I love you so mu—"

When his voice caught, he began kissing her neck. Then he took her mouth, his scent and taste invading her system, building fires, inflaming desires that had been stored too long.

Suddenly the horses took offense to being in such close proximity to each other and wheeled, almost throwing their riders onto the ground. Pip yelped, caught in the shuffle. Nick gave that irrepressible laugh of his, his dark eyes alight with fire that equaled Carla's. "Let's go find somewhere special to finish this."

"I think I know just the place." She wheeled Molly and galloped up the trail toward the northwest.

They tethered the horses in the meadow and ordered their bodyguard to stay, then walked into the pine grove. The trees were glowing in the sunset. Excited sighs and murmurs wafted in their boughs and curled around the cabin, reaching out to Carla and Nick. "Don't laugh. I know I'm being ridiculously silly," she said softly, "but it feels like Emily is welcoming us."

Enfolding her in his arms, Nick rubbed his cheek against Carla's short hair. "I love it when you're being ridiculously silly. But how do you know it's not Michel?"

"Or both," Carla whispered, curving her body to fit against his from knees to shoulders. "I came here often while you were gone. I cried when I discovered you'd fixed up the cabin, the monument to our beginning. I thought it was all over for us."

"How could it have been . . . ? Remember, we're fated." He lifted his head and looked down into her face, smiling. "Want to know the real reason I fixed it up?"

"Why?" she whispered, loving him so much, she felt she would surely burst.

"Because it's a perfect place to ask—" He stopped as if something had strangled him; a panicked look invaded his eyes. A rare, total, expectant silence fell around the trees and the cabin as Nick bit his upper lip, struggling with himself.

Carla held him tightly in her arms, understanding how hard it was for her ramblin' man to make the biggest commitment of all. "It doesn't matter, darling. I don't need to hear the words. I'm yours forever, whether you say it or not."

"No, I want to so badly, I have to say it." His dark eyes bathed her with glowing love. The words were a husky whisper when they came. "If you're still looking for a forever man . . . will you marry me?"

Putting one hand on either side of his face, Carla answered in a quavery voice. "Yes, darling, a thousand times yes, I'll marry you."

A triumphant sigh trembled in the trees.

"Oh, sweetheart, Carla, you've made me so happy. I love you more than anything else in this fascinating world."

Bending his head, he scattered scalding kisses up her neck and on her mouth until he'd brought her body to aching life. His face was soft with desire when he lifted his head. She looked up and smiled. "Don't you think this would be a perfect place to consummate our marriage . . . Nicky?"

He laughed softly, laying her down on the carpet of pine needles, among the wildflowers. "I can't think of a more perfect place in all the world, sweetheart."

Later, sated and happy, Carla pillowed her head on his shoulder and stared blissfully at the pine boughs wafting in the breeze. Something seemed odd, but she couldn't put her finger on it. Then she realized what it was. "Nick, listen!"

"Hmmm?" He glanced contentedly around, then tightened his arms around her and nestled her closer. "I don't hear anything."

"That's what I mean. The only sound is the breeze in the boughs. The whispers are gone."

He lifted his head and bent a more serious ear to listening. "You're right. Guess that must mean Emily and Michel are finally at peace, huh?" Dropping his head back down, he flashed that cocky grin she loved so much. "Now we know why fate brought us together—to write a happy ending onto their love story."

"Oh, you and your fate!" Carla exclaimed, then stared into his face, frowning skeptically. "You don't really, *really* believe in lingering traces or fate, do you?"

"Mm-m-m . . . ," he answered, and drove the matter out of her mind with his lips.

THE EDITOR'S CORNER

Next month LOVESWEPT salutes **MEN IN UNIFORM**, those daring heroes who risk all for life, liberty . . . and the pursuit of women they desire. **MEN IN UNIFORM** are experts at plotting seductive maneuvers, and in six fabulous romances, you'll be at the front lines of passion as each of these men wages a battle for the heart of the woman he loves.

The first of our dashing heroes is Brett Upton in **JUST FRIENDS** by Laura Taylor, LOVESWEPT #600—and he's furious about the attack on Leah Holbrook's life, the attack that cost her her memory and made her forget the love they'd once shared and that he'd betrayed. Now, as he desperately guards her, he dares to believe that fate has given him a second chance to win back the only woman he's ever wanted. Laura will hold you spellbound with this powerful romance.

In **FLYBOY** by Victoria Leigh, LOVESWEPT #601, veteran Air Force pilot Matt Cooper has seen plenty of excitement, but nothing compares to the storm of desire he feels when he rescues Jennifer Delaney from a raging typhoon. Matt has always called the world his home, but the redhead suddenly makes him long to settle down. And with wildfire embraces and whispers of passionate fantasies, he sets out to make the independent beauty share his newfound dream. A splendid love story, told with plenty of Victoria's wit.

Patricia Potter returns to LOVESWEPT with **TROUBA-DOUR,** LOVESWEPT #602. Connor MacLaren is fiercely masculine in a kilt—and from the moment she first lays eyes on him, Leslie Turner feels distinctly overwhelmed. Hired as a publicist for the touring folk-singer, she'd expected anything except this rugged Scot who awakens a reckless hunger she'd never dare con-fess. But armed with a killer grin and potent kisses, Connor vows to make her surrender to desire. You'll treasure this enchanting romance from Pat.

In her new LOVESWEPT, **HART'S LAW,** #603, Theresa Gladden gives us a sexy sheriff whose smile can melt steel. When Johnny Hart hears that Bailey Asher's coming home, he remembers kissing her breathless the summer she was seventeen—and wonders if she'd still feel so good in his embrace. But Bailey no longer trusts men and she insists on keeping her distance. How Johnny convinces her to open her arms—and heart—to him once more makes for one of Theresa's best LOVESWEPTs.

SURRENDER, BABY, LOVESWEPT #604 by Suzanne Forster, is Geoff Dias's urgent message to Miranda Witherspoon. A soldier of fortune, Geoff has seen and done it all, but nothing burns in his memory more than that one night ten years ago when he'd tasted fierce passion in Miranda's arms. When he agrees to help her find her missing fiancé, he has just one objective in mind: to make her see they're destined only for each other. The way Suzanne writes, the sexual sparks practically leap off the page!

Finally, in **HEALING TOUCH** by Judy Gill, LOVESWEPT #605, army doctor Rob McGee needs a wife to help him raise his young orphaned niece—but what he wants is

Heather Tomasi! He met the lovely temptress only once two years before, but his body still remembers the silk of her skin and the wicked promises in her eyes. She's definitely not marriage material, but Rob has made up his mind. And he'll do anything—even bungee jump—to prove to her that he's the man she needs. Judy will delight you with this wonderful tale.

On sale this month from FANFARE are four fabulous novels. From highly acclaimed author Deborah Smith comes **BLUE WILLOW,** a gloriously heart-stopping love story with characters as passionate and bold as the South that brought them forth. Artemas Colebrook and Lily MacKenzie are bound to each other through the Blue Willow estate . . . and by a passion that could destroy all they have struggled for.

The superstar of the sensual historical, Susan Johnson tempts you with **SINFUL.** Set in the 1780s, Chelsea Ferguson must escape a horrible fate—marriage to a man she doesn't love—by bedding another man. But Sinjin St. John, Duke of Seth, refuses to be her rescuer and Chelsea must resort to a desperate deception that turns into a passionate adventure.

Bestselling LOVESWEPT author Helen Mittermeyer has penned **THE PRINCESS OF THE VEIL,** a breathtakingly romantic tale set in long-ago Scotland and Iceland. When Viking princess Iona is captured by the notorious Scottish chief Magnus Sinclair, she vows never to belong to him, though he would make her his bride.

Theresa Weir, author of the widely praised **FOREVER,** delivers a new novel of passion and drama. In **LAST SUMMER,** movie star Johnnie Irish returns to his Texas hometown, intent on getting revenge. But all thoughts of getting even disappear when he meets the beautiful widow Maggie Mayfield.

Also on sale this month in the hardcover edition from Doubleday is **SACRED LIES** by Dianne Edouard and Sandra Ware. In this sexy contemporary novel, Romany Chase must penetrate the inner sanctum of the Vatican on a dangerous mission . . . and walk a fine line between two men who could be friend or foe.

Happy reading!

With warmest wishes,

Nita Taublib

Nita Taublib
Associate Publisher
LOVESWEPT and FANFARE

OFFICIAL RULES TO WINNERS CLASSIC SWEEPSTAKES

No Purchase necessary. To enter the sweepstakes follow instructions found elsewhere in this offer. You can also enter the sweepstakes by hand printing your name, address, city, state and zip code on a 3" x 5" piece of paper and mailing it to: Winners Classic Sweepstakes, P.O. Box 785, Gibbstown, NJ 08027. Mail each entry separately. Sweepstakes begins 12/1/91. Entries must be received by 6/1/93. Some presentations of this sweepstakes may feature a deadline for the Early Bird prize. If the offer you receive does, then to be eligible for the Early Bird prize your entry must be received according to the Early Bird date specified. Not responsible for lost, late, damaged, misdirected, illegible or postage due mail. Mechanically reproduced entries are not eligible. All entries become property of the sponsor and will not be returned.

Prize Selection/Validations: Winners will be selected in random drawings on or about 7/30/93, by VENTURA ASSOCIATES, INC., an independent judging organization whose decisions are final. Odds of winning are determined by total number of entries received. Circulation of this sweepstakes is estimated not to exceed 200 million. Entrants need not be present to win. All prizes are guaranteed to be awarded and delivered to winners. Winners will be notified by mail and may be required to complete the affidavit of eligibility and release of liability which must be returned within 14 days of date of notification or alternate winners will be selected. Any guest of a trip winner will also be required to execute a release of liability. Any prize notification letter or any prize returned to a participating sponsor, Bantam Doubleday Dell Publishing Group, Inc., its participating divisions or subsidiaries, or VENTURA ASSOCIATES, INC. as undeliverable will be awarded to an alternate winner. Prizes are not transferable. No multiple prize winners except as may be necessary due to unavailability, in which case a prize of equal or greater value will be awarded. Prizes will be awarded approximately 90 days after the drawing. All taxes, automobile license and registration fees, if applicable, are the sole responsibility of the winners. Entry constitutes permission (except where prohibited) to use winners' names and likenesses for publicity purposes without further or other compensation.

Participation: This sweepstakes is open to residents of the United States and Canada, except for the province of Quebec. This sweepstakes is sponsored by Bantam Doubleday Dell Publishing Group, Inc. (BDD), 666 Fifth Avenue, New York, NY 10103. Versions of this sweepstakes with different graphics will be offered in conjunction with various solicitations or promotions by different subsidiaries and divisions of BDD. Employees and their families of BDD, its division, subsidiaries, advertising agencies, and VENTURA ASSOCIATES, INC., are not eligible.

Canadian residents, in order to win, must first correctly answer a time limited arithmetical skill testing question. Void in Quebec and wherever prohibited or restricted by law. Subject to all federal, state, local and provincial laws and regulations.

Prizes: The following values for prizes are determined by the manufacturers' suggested retail prices or by what these items are currently known to be selling for at the time this offer was published. Approximate retail values include handling and delivery of prizes. Estimated maximum retail value of prizes: 1 Grand Prize ($27,500 if merchandise or $25,000 Cash); 1 First Prize ($3,000); 5 Second Prizes ($400 each); 35 Third Prizes ($100 each); 1,000 Fourth Prizes ($9.00 each) ; 1 Early Bird Prize ($5,000); Total approximate maximum retail value is $50,000. Winners will have the option of selecting any prize offered at level won. Automobile winner must have a valid driver's license at the time the car is awarded. Trips are subject to space and departure availability. Certain black-out dates may apply. Travel must be completed within one year from the time the prize is awarded. Minors must be accompanied by an adult. Prizes won by minors will be awarded in the name of parent or legal guardian.

For a list of Major Prize Winners (available after 7/30/93): send a self-addressed, stamped envelope entirely separate from your entry to: Winners Classic Sweepstakes Winners, P.O. Box 825, Gibbstown, NJ 08027. Requests must be received by 6/1/93. DO NOT SEND ANY OTHER CORRESPONDENCE TO THIS P.O. BOX.

SWP 9/92

Women's Fiction

On Sale in January

BLUE WILLOW

29690-6 $5.50/6.50 in Canada

☐

by Deborah Smith

Bestselling author of MIRACLE

*"Extraordinary talent.... A complex and emotionally wrenching tale
that sweeps the readers on an intense rollercoaster ride through
the gamut of human emotions."* —*Romantic Times*

SINFUL

9312-5 $4.99/5.99 in Canada

☐

by Susan Johnson

Author of FORBIDDEN

*"The author's style is a pleasure to read and the love scenes
many and lusty!"* —*Los Angeles Herald Examiner*

PRINCESS OF THE VEIL

29581-0 $4.99/5.99 in Canada

☐

by Helen Mittermeyer

*"Intrigue, a fascinating setting, high adventure, a wonderful love
story and steamy sensuality."* —*Romantic Times*

LAST SUMMER

56092-1 $4.99/5.99 in Canada

☐

by Theresa Weir

Author of FOREVER

*"An exceptional new talent...a splendid adventure that will delight
readers with its realistic background and outstanding sexual
tension."* —*Rave Reviews*

☐ Please send me the books I have checked above I am enclosing $ _____ (add $2.50 to cover
postage and handling) Send check or money order, no cash or C. O. D.'s please.

Name _____

Address _____

City/ State/ Zip _____

Send order to: Bantam Books, Dept FN93, 2451 S Wolf Rd., Des Plaines, IL 60018

Allow four to six weeks for delivery Prices and availability subject to change without notice.

Ask for these books at your local bookstore or use this page to order.   FN93 2/93

Women's Fiction

On Sale in February

TEMPERATURES RISING

56054-X $5.99/6.99 in Canada

☐ **by Sandra Brown**

New York Times bestselling author of
A WHOLE NEW LIGHT and FRENCH SILK

A contemporary tale of love and passion in the South Pacific

OUTLAW HEARTS

29807-0 $5.50/6.50 in Canada

☐ **by Rosanne Bittner**

Bestselling author of SONG OF THE WOLF,
praised by *Romantic Times* as "a stunning
achievement...that moves the soul and fills the heart."

THE LAST HIGHWAYMAN

56065-4 $5.50/6.50 in Canada

☐ **by Katherine O'Neal**

Fascinating historical fact and sizzling romantic fiction meet
in this sensual tale of a legendary bandit and a scandalous
high-born lady.

CONFIDENCES

56170-7 $4.99/5.99 in Canada

☐ **by Penny Hayden**

"Thirtysomething" meets Danielle Steel—four best friends
are bound by an explosive secret.

Ask for these books at your local bookstore or use this page to order.

☐ Please send me the books I have checked above. I am enclosing $ _____ (add $2.50
to cover postage and handling). Send check or money order, no cash or C. O. D.'s please.

Name _____

Address _____

City/ State/ Zip _____

Send order to: Bantam Books, Dept. FN94, 2451 S. Wolf Rd., Des Plaines, IL 60018
Allow four to six weeks for delivery.

Prices and availability subject to change without notice.   FN94 2/93

⚞FANFARE

Bestselling Women's Fiction

Sandra Brown

_____	29783-X	A WHOLE NEW LIGHT ..... $5.99/6.99 in Canada
_____	29500-4	TEXAS! SAGE $4.99/5.99
_____	29085-1	22 INDIGO PLACE $4.50/5.50
_____	28990-X	TEXAS! CHASE $4.99/5.99
_____	28951-9	TEXAS! LUCKY $4.99/5.99

Amanda Quick

_____	29325-7	RENDEZVOUS $4.99/5.99
_____	28354-5	SEDUCTION $4.99/5.99
_____	28932-2	SCANDAL $4.95/5.95
_____	28594-7	SURRENDER $4.50/5.50

Nora Roberts

_____	29597-7	CARNAL INNOCENCE $5.50/6.50
_____	29078-9	GENUINE LIES $4.99/5.99
_____	28578-5	PUBLIC SECRETS $4.95/5.95
_____	26461-3	HOT ICE $4.99/5.99
_____	26574-1	SACRED SINS $5.50/6.50
_____	27859-2	SWEET REVENGE $5.50/6.50
_____	27283-7	BRAZEN VIRTUE $4.99/5.99

Iris Johansen

_____	29871-2	LAST BRIDGE HOME $4.50/5.50
_____	29604-3	THE GOLDEN BARBARIAN $4.99/5.99
_____	29244-7	REAP THE WIND $4.99/5.99
_____	29032-0	STORM WINDS $4.99/5.99
_____	28855-5	THE WIND DANCER............................. $4.95/5.95

Ask for these titles at your bookstore or use this page to order.

Please send me the books I have checked above. I am enclosing $ _____ (add $2.50 to
cover postage and handling). Send check or money order, no cash or C. O. D.'s please.

Mr./ Ms. _____

Address _____

City/ State/ Zip _____

Send order to: Bantam Books, Dept. FN 16, 2451 S. Wolf Road, Des Plaines, IL 60018
Please allow four to six weeks for delivery.

Prices and availability subject to change without notice.   FN 16 - 8/92